Alien Prince's Secret Baby

Olympus Station, Volume 2

Aurelia Skye

Published by Amourisa Press, 2019.

Blurb

AS THE SECOND-IN-COMMAND of Olympus Station, Captain Hadley Wells is usually too focused on her career to worry about romance. That changes with the arrival of Prince Nykal of Jroj, a planet that's recently joined the Coalition. Their attraction is immediate and fierce, but too many rules separate them to let them have more than one stolen night. The night is amazing, but has far-reaching consequences. Add in the ambassador determined to keep Nykal from her by any means, and it's a complicated mess that needs a solution before the secret she carries is visible to all.

Chapter One

HADLEY RAN AS FAST as she could until she reached the bend in the corridor that would bring her in view of the alien prince and ambassador awaiting her attention. At that point, she slowed to a stop, took a deep breath, and smoothed her uniform before stepping into sight and walking toward them at a more sedate pace. She could see Krill's curl of the lip, which indicated he was disappointed to see her instead of Weston. Her gaze flicked to the prince, and Nykal's obvious appreciation warmed her. It was clear he preferred having her to Weston.

"Where's the commander, Captain Wells?" Krill spoke in a clipped way that suggested he had little time to spare for her.

She forced a pleasant smile to remain on her face. "He's with…" She trailed off for a moment, uncertain how to identify Piper. His surrogate? She really didn't want to delve into the ugly history between Piper and her twin sister Pippa, who had been married to the commander until her death recently.

She settled for saying, "There's been an emergency with the mother of his child. That was why he had to run earlier, and thank you for understanding why we had to cut short the meeting. He's asked me to fill in for him for now, so I'll be leading you on a tour of Olympus Station."

Krill looked put out, but Nykal's grin seemed to transmit he was happy to see her. The smile made his already handsome, if intense, face less intimidating. She'd barely interacted with the prince yet, but he seemed fairly approachable anyway. It was difficult not to stare at him, though she had seen many aliens in her career as second-in-command of one of the Coalition's main outposts.

The Jroj were a relatively recent addition to the Coalition, and their language database hadn't even been fully integrated into the Coalition's yet. They were humanoid, but faintly exotic with their light-orange skin and the faintest ripple of black stripes throughout. Their skin reminded her of the extinct Earth tiger, which someone had pointed out in the briefing manuals she and Weston had received from the Coalition headquarters before the ambassador and prince's arrival. The pattern was much subtler than a tiger's though, and Nykal didn't seem to have same kind of killer instinct that appeared in images she'd seen of tigers.

She shivered slightly when she accidentally met Krill's gaze. *He* did seem to have that same kind of cold edge that suggested he wasn't above predation. She tried not to have a negative opinion of him, especially since the ambassador was going to be stationed permanently on Olympus, but she hadn't liked him from the moment they met earlier.

"Please lead the way, Captain Wells."

She couldn't help a warm smile for the prince. "Please feel free to call me Hadley, Your Highness."

He nodded. "In that case, I insist you call me Nykal."

Krill cleared his throat. "That would be a breach of protocol, Your Highness."

Nykal shrugged in a careless fashion before lowering his voice to a conspiratorial whisper. "I won't tell if you don't, Krill."

He stepped closer to Hadley, holding out his hand with the palm facing downward. She remembered that was an invitation to walk with him, and she reciprocated by putting her palm faceup against his hand, so the backs of their hands touched. The gesture felt awkward, but she couldn't deny a shiver of awareness went down her spine at the simple touch.

She giggled a moment later when Nykal added in a pseudo-whisper, "I'm sure he won't keep that to himself. Ambassador Krill is a stickler for decorum and etiquette. I'm probably currently being written up, with my transgressions broadcast to Parliament."

Though there was a teasing note in his voice, his gaze was unexpectedly serious for a moment before he seemed to mentally shrug it all aside. "What is this place?"

She showed him the level by extending her arm. "This is where we have our merchant shops, along with some eateries, and entertainment. We have a VR platform that's a favorite amongst those seeking recreation."

"Impressive. That's technology we don't have, though I've seen it mentioned in the notes."

"Have you had to do much studying for your trip, Your Highness? I mean Nykal?"

Nykal didn't get a chance to answer before Krill said, "There's been much study to prepare for our Coalition application, along with this visit. We studied the Coalition, and the aliens who form it for solar cycles, even before we began doing business with the Coalition, and long before we decided it would be strategically wise to join the union."

She nodded politely at Krill's response, though her question had been addressed to Nykal. She got the sense he wasn't one to enjoy sitting down and reading boring paper after paper. Or maybe she was simply projecting her own preferences onto him. She had done hours of study in preparation for this visit and the ambassador's arrival as well, but it was one of the more tedious aspects of her job.

She led them through the station, pointing out various places of interest. She made an effort to keep it professional and semiformal, but Nykal seemed determined to make it more like a friendly meeting than an official function. He made jokes and asked personal questions, but not so personal that they crossed the line. It quickly became obvious he wanted to know if she was involved with anyone, and he was trying to find that information by asking things like what color uniform her betrothed wore.

She spent a few minutes tapdancing around the questions, enjoying teasing him lightly with pretended obliviousness, before finally admitting, "I don't have a betrothed, or a partner. My duties on Olympus Station keep me much too busy."

Nykal heaved a sigh. "I understand that." He turned away from her to scan the room. "And what is this facility?"

She gestured to the five-story platform. "This houses our oxygen scrubbers, which keep us all alive—except for the Denarii ambassador, who has to wear a rebreather everywhere but her quarters."

Nykal seemed fascinated. "What's a Denarii?"

She held her hand about three meters high to indicate height. "The ambassador is about this tall, light pink, and covered with fuzz. She requires a much higher concentration of nitrogen than humans and most other humanoids in the Coalition, but her quarters are kept separate from the station to maintain the proper ratio for her, so she isn't required to wear the rebreather all the time."

"That's interesting. How—"

Krill interrupted the prince's question. "While we would like to discuss an ambassadorship, I have no intention of wasting time discussing the Denarii ambassador," said Krill in a stern voice. "Show me where my quarters will be, along with my workspace."

As Nykal sighed, she almost reminded him to use his manners, but then realized that Jroj might not use common courtesies like "please and thank you," or even know how to ask nicely—though the prince seemed to have far better manners, so she was probably giving Krill too much benefit of the doubt.

She nodded at him and led them from the oxygen-scrubbing room, seeing no need to take them through the intricacies of the system or tour each of the five levels that comprised the area. They took the lift system up a few floors to the diplomatic sector, where various ambassadors and embassies shared workspace. Their permanent living quarters were on the floor above.

The first sight when they stepped out of the lift was a clear wall that afforded them a view of the stars around them. It was a breathtaking sight that rarely failed to catch Hadley's attention, even if it was just for a few moments in the process of doing other errands. Today, she barely glanced at it, focused as she was on appeasing Krill.

Nykal apparently didn't share that concern, because he paused and moved closer to the wall, placing a palm against it. "It's quite humbling, isn't it?"

She frowned. "I beg your pardon?"

"To see how small we are in the scheme of things, I mean. That's humbling. Olympus Station is quite sizable, approximately the size of one of our smaller cities, if my research hasn't failed me, yet seems minuscule when compared to the vastness of space."

She smiled at the poetry of his words and nodded. "I guess it is humbling. I haven't thought about it that way before, but you're right. Don't you have such a view from your planet?"

"The prince rightly stays mostly in the palace, Captain Wells. It isn't safe for him to venture out."

She forced a pleasant smile for Ambassador Krill, but couldn't imagine having to live that way. It was true she was technically trapped on Olympus Station, limited to escape only on her vacation times, but it never felt like she was imprisoned. She couldn't imagine being anywhere else, and she loved the place down to its last nut and bolt.

"Unfortunately, we don't have any windows like this in the palace, but I might insist upon having one installed," said Nykal with a small sigh before turning away from the view.

Hadley took that as her cue to continue the tour, so she led them down the corridor, turning twice, before approaching the office that was labeled with Ambassador Krill's name. She used her biometric print to open it, gesturing for them to come inside. "Do you know how to reprogram the biometric panel to recognize your authority, Ambassador Krill?"

The other man nodded, but wasn't really looking at her as he can glanced around his office. He sniffed lightly. "I assumed it would be larger."

Somehow, she held her patience and gritted her teeth as she led him to another door, which revealed a larger workspace. "This is for your use, and the first room is for any staff you might wish to bring with you."

He didn't look grateful or even annoyed. He just seemed rather neutral. "This will be adequate. Thank you, Captain. Now if you'll excuse us, the prince and I have things to discuss before our next meeting with the commander." He frowned slightly. "I trust the commander will be at our next meeting?"

Hadley couldn't stifle the urge to shrug, which wasn't particularly professional. She straightened her spine and stood straighter. "I'm not entirely certain, Ambassador Krill. It depends on his personal situation. As you can imagine, his family is his top priority."

Ambassador Krill shook his head. "That's always a failing among those in power. One can't effectively lead if their focus is divided between personal problems and far more important matters of state, or in the case of the station, security."

She tightened her hands into fists, but somehow managed to keep her tone sounding pleasant. "I'll be certain to relay that to him. Please call me if you need anything, and otherwise, I'll be back to escort you to dinner."

"I'm sure that won't be necessary, Captain." Krill was staring thoughtfully at the prince as he said the words. "If the commander is unavailable to dine with us as protocol establishes, we'll simply have something in our rooms."

Nykal frowned. "I prefer to go out and see more of the station."

Krill frowned. "You've had an adequate tour from the second-in-command, Your Highness. Protocol dictates the safe and wise course is to stay in your quarters until the next official function. By my count, that will be the reception—unless I'm mistaken, Captain Wells?"

Hadley briefly glanced at her wrist comm, though she had the schedule memorized. "That's correct, Ambassador Krill."

The ambassador nodded his darker orange head, which was bald instead of covered by the glossy brown hair decorating Nykal's. "In that case, I see no reason for us to disturb you until then."

With her mouth compressed tightly, she nodded to both before dismissing herself, though she'd already been sent away through Krill's manner. He made it obvious he wanted nothing to do with her, or at least as little as possible. When it came to the ambassador, that suited her just fine, but she was disappointed not to have a reason to spend more time with the prince.

SHE WAS SURPRISED TO receive a personal message later that evening, and even more surprised to see the prince's face on her vid screen when she accepted the call. "May I assist you in some way, Your Highness?" She wondered if the A.I. had rerouted the call to her if it had been meant for Weston. The last she'd heard from Weston, he would probably be occupied with Piper's health up until the day of the reception, so he might have shut off vid call functions.

"I thought we might sneak out to sample the VR platform?" He spoke in a teasing, yet enticing, fashion.

She couldn't hide her delight at the idea, feeling naughty and fully enjoying it. "What will Ambassador Krill say?"

"Hopefully, he'll say nothing, because he'll never know. If he finds out, it will be just another lecture to endure on *etiquette* and *protocol*." He said the two words like they were something foul. "I might as well enjoy it if I'm going to be punished anyway, so are you up for acting as my guide, Hadley?"

She nodded, not admitting she was up for far more than that. "I'd be honored, Nykal."

"I hate to be a bother, but would you mind coming to my quarters to meet me, so I don't get lost?"

Hadley nodded. "Not a problem, but if you do get lost at some point while on the station, any of the kiosks located every few hundred feet offer information to orient yourself, and there's always the communication system. Our A.I. can guide you wherever you need to go."

"That's good to know. I'll see you soon."

With that, his image disappeared from the screen, and she turned it off.

Hadley started to the door, but froze when she looked down. She still wore her gray uniform. That wasn't exactly flattering, so she spent five minutes trading it for more casual clothing that was formfitting and didn't scream matronly aunt. After that, she rushed to the prince's quarters and tapped lightly on the door, half-afraid Krill was listening from his room next door and waiting to pounce on her at the slightest sign of interaction with the Prince.

To her relief, the panel slid open to reveal the prince, with no sign of Krill, and he stepped out to join her in the corridor. He'd shed the ornate black robe thing he'd worn before, and the lightweight crown that had been on his head was also gone. There was nothing overtly princely about him, though he was still charming and far too appealing for her common sense.

"You look far more relaxed." That was a too-forward thing to say, and she blushed as she murmured it.

"As do you." He reached out, lightly caressing her hair. "It's longer than I expected."

Hadley had forgotten she'd taken down the light-brown mass from its customary roll upon reentering her quarters after her shift ended. It hung around her face and down her back. "I keep thinking I'll cut it someday, but never have the time." Or the courage, since she happened to like her long hair. It wasn't strictly Coalition-standard, but no one objected as long as she kept it pinned up.

They chatted like old friends, and things were easy and peaceful between them even on such short acquaintance, as they made their way to the VR platform. There was a small line, and she started to move to the front to supersede those waiting on diplomatic grounds. She froze when Nykal put a hand on her arm, arresting her progress.

"Please don't inconvenience others on my behalf. I prefer we wait our turn, unless you're in a rush?"

She shook her head. "I don't mind waiting." If she got to spend more time with the handsome Jrojan prince, how could she mind?

"I haven't done anything this normal in several solar cycles."

She frowned. "You mean wait in line?"

He nodded. "There were many occurrences where the middle son had to wait in line, and I wasn't fawned over and treated with the same obsequiousness as my older brother, Mygal."

The name was familiar, and she struggled to remember where she'd heard it before. The knowledge came back to her suddenly when she recalled the Crown Prince of the Jrojan Empire had died in an accident ten solar cycles before. "You weren't expecting to inherit the throne, were you?"

He shook his head. "Not at all. There isn't a lot of freedom in the life of a Minor Royal Prince, but I was practically free to do anything I wished in comparison to the life I have now, after having the yoke of leadership thrust upon me. It's quite restrictive, and there's little room for fun."

"That sounds miserable." She bit her tongue, wondering if she should've been so blunt with her opinion.

He shrugged. "It certainly isn't what I planned, and it's unfortunate that the line of succession requires me to fill Mygal's place, because my younger brother, Vasar, would be a far more suitable king than I'll ever make."

The line had moved, and it was almost their turn now. "I'm sorry you're unhappy with your role, Nykal."

He shrugged. "It could always be worse." He managed a melancholy smile, but all that seemed to melt away when it was finally their turn a few minutes later. He was as excited as her little sister had always been on Christmas morning. The prince was practically bouncing in place with anticipation, which she found endearing—and also made it difficult not to laugh.

She approached the panel to scan her hand. "What kind of experience would you like?"

He bit his lip, looking indecisive. "I'm not sure. What do you suggest?"

"Some people enjoy sports recreation. There's a program that allows you to climb the Matterhorn, which is a high mountain on Earth. Or you can visit the Anjovian planes, which are so perfectly flat they can be used to calibrate levels. That's a tool that tells one if they're hanging an object straight."

He shrugged. "There's so much of the universe I haven't seen that I don't know where to begin. You choose."

After a brief hesitation, she selected Senufo. They stepped inside, and the room was blank for a moment as it loaded the Senufo program. A moment later, the replica of the planet flickered into view. "This is the place I love, Nykal."

"It's amazing." His eyes seemed as wide as saucers when he took in the areas of blank space between crystals of various sizes and colors. They were all naturally occurring, and though she'd never been on the Senufo home world, she was certain the VR platform offered an authentic replica.

She moved to one of the crystals that appeared to be growing from the floor, which was configured into the natural formation of stone, complete with irregular cracks and dips. Hadley sat down, patting the section beside her, and the prince joined her.

She pointed upward, and his mouth fell open again when he saw the stars above them. Senufo was in a particularly active section of its galaxy, and meteors streaked across the sky almost continuously. Everything had a faintly purple-green glow, though the crystals came in a variety of colors.

She instinctively relaxed. This was her favorite place and secret refuge. She'd never brought anyone here before.

As though he sensed that, he turned to face her, taking her hand in his. "Thank you for sharing this private moment with me, Hadley."

She shrugged a shoulder. "It's no problem, Nykal. I enjoy being able to share it with someone."

She thought he might kiss her, and she was certainly prepared to let him despite all the rules forbidding them from getting involved. It wasn't strictly Coalition policy, because there was nothing written down to address the situation either way, but she had received a book that filled much of the memory capacity of her datapad. It had encompassed all the rules by which the Jroj lived.

Among those was an embargo on propagating outside one's species, which automatically led to Jrojs being technically forbidden to date or romantically interact with any species but their own. With him being the Crown Prince, there were even more rules in place. Sitting here privately holding his hand, without a proper chaperone, was probably breaking at least five of them. She couldn't summon the energy to care at present. It felt too lovely to sit there beside the prince, his hand in hers, while they stared up at the lightshow sparkling above them.

When it was over, and he indicated he must return, she walked him back to his room and left him there. It took everything she had not to lean forward to kiss him, and she detected he was fighting the same battle himself. She was disappointed when he appeared to win it, and she forced herself to take a step back. She nodded her head at him. "I'll see you at the reception, if not before, Nykal."

He looked sad for a moment. "Yes, and thank you for this evening. It's something I'll never forget. You're someone I'll never forget." That seemed to be as close as he could come to any formal declaration of how he was feeling.

She understood the stoicism that kept any other declarations locked inside, and she wasn't about to verbally admit her attraction either. She doubted her body could hide it as well as her mind or face could. She simply nodded to him and took another step back, pressing the button on the outside that closed the panel. She needed the barrier between them to keep herself from crossing over the boundary and stepping into his room.

If she stepped into his world even marginally, she was certain it would be impossible to leave easily. She doubted she would even want to if it just involved the prince. She wanted him with a hunger she wasn't sure could be assuaged, and a need she couldn't quite explain. It wasn't just sexual. She was sure of that.

While she walked back to her quarters, she tried to analyze every second of the interaction between them, continuously returning to the tender instants they'd shared in silence, just holding hands and finding a peaceful moment to bask in each other. Even if that was all she ever got with the prince, it would be enough to fuel her most decadent fantasies. The memory would have to tide her over when she thought about him—and she was afraid she would spend far too much time thinking about Prince Nykal in the coming days.

Chapter Two

THE NEXT FEW DAYS WERE a whirlwind of activity for Hadley, since Weston was still with Piper as she recovered from her near-loss of the baby. Hadley stepped in and handled most of Weston's tasks, which should have brought her in more contact with Nykal, but didn't. Krill seemed determined to wait on Weston, though he made his impatience clear each time he spoke with her, requesting Weston present himself. Hadley always promised to pass along the message, and she did so, but Weston continued to make the right choice by staying with the mother of his child.

To her disappointment, she'd only seen the prince once in passing over the last couple of days, and he'd had Krill in tow. That had severely curtailed their interaction, which had consisted solely of polite generalities, and there'd been no opportunity to discuss anything more personal.

Nights were a different matter. He filled her mind from the time she laid down until she fell asleep. He'd spurred more than one passionate fantasy that ended with her bringing herself to satisfaction. That felt empty and hollow, but she couldn't stop thinking about him and turning herself on to the point where she needed to find relief. She wanted to be with him, though she knew how impractical that was.

Finally, it was the night of the reception, and she hoped she might have a chance to interact more normally with him. Weston had already alerted her that he and Piper would be in attendance, and she knew he'd spent part of the afternoon dealing with Krill. That meant he was likely to need several strong drinks.

She put on her dress uniform, which was about as exciting as her matronly aunt regular uniform, but it couldn't be helped. As much as she'd like to wear something prettier, she couldn't break protocol. As an officer on the station, she had to represent Olympus with proper decorum.

As she walked to the reception, she realized Nykal was probably in a similar situation. He was forced to represent Jroj despite how uncomfortable it might make him. Perhaps she was imagining things, but it seemed like he wore the crown with a heavy head. Considering he hadn't expected to inherit the title, it was no surprise he seemed to be chafing under the restrictions.

When she reached the reception, the first person she saw was Nykal, seated beside Krill as a guest of honor at the main table. Piper and Weston also sat there, and Piper looked much better. Hadley paused to ask her friend in a low voice, "How are you feeling?"

Piper smiled up at her. "I feel much better now. Thank you."

With a nod, Hadley moved on to take her seat beside Weston, which just happened to put her across the table from Nykal. She flashed him a brighter smile than she probably should before turning to look at Krill. She nodded her head. "Ambassador Krill." Then she looked back at Nykal. "How are you this evening, Prince Nykal?" Though he'd given permission for her to use his first name, she still wanted a touch of decorum under the circumstances.

His lips twitched, and he seemed to understand why she'd introduced the level of formality between them. "I'm doing very well, Captain Wells. How are you this evening?"

"I'm well, thank you." Hadley waited a little while, not speaking until after they'd eaten, and Krill had Weston immersed in conversation that seemed to revolve around the exact cubic centimeters of his office versus the space reserved for the Enboriguy ambassador. Krill seem to think his space was ten centimeters less.

She couldn't resist rolling her eyes at that, and her gaze caught Nykal's. Since Krill was currently immersed in his petty complaints, she nodded her head toward the dance floor, where couples were starting to gather. She quirked a brow, and Nykal nodded. She slipped away first, feeling as though they were sneaking around like a couple of teenagers. That enhanced the thrill just a little bit, but she also didn't like having to do so. It was ridiculous that layers of protocol and decorum kept them from being able to openly approach the dance floor without rancor from Krill.

He met her a couple of moments later, holding out his hand. This time, the palm was faceup, and she took it the usual way. Holding on to him, she put her other hand on his shoulder, and his went to her waist.

"I must warn you I've only had a little time to study Coalition dances. It might shock you to know the Jroj don't dance."

Hadley giggled. "No, I'd never guess that."

"I think most of the older Jroj have forgotten how to have fun, if they ever knew. They seem determined to wear down the younger generation the moment we try something different." He looked sad for a moment, but then he blinked. "But that's a discussion for another time, when I don't have a beautiful woman in my arms."

Her cheeks flushed with pleasure from his words. "Will Krill give you hell for this?" She closed her eyes as she realized she'd just cursed in front of the prince. "I apologize for the language. That wasn't very professional of me."

"I'm not entirely certain what it means, but I take it one of those words is inappropriate?" She nodded. "In that case, feel free to use it at length and leisure whenever you're around me." He winked at her. "Dancing is already illicit, so I might as well make it completely forbidden."

"By cursing?" she asked with her eyes wide.

He shrugged a shoulder. "I was thinking something far riskier and more personal." He closed some of the distance between them, taking their dance from proper to bordering on improper. That allowed his mouth to be near her ear when he whispered, "Will you come to my quarters later tonight?"

She stiffened, pulling away to look up at him. She couldn't blatantly ask what he wanted, but she doubted it was simply a social visit. "Would you like me to come by for a nightcap?"

A slow, wicked grin transformed his expression. "That and more. I apologize for being so forward, but as you know, I'll be leaving tomorrow. This is our last chance. I have absolutely no anger if you're unable to come, because I understand the risk to your career. I'm taking a risk as well, but the idea of leaving here without ever holding you beyond the way we're dancing now seems like a crime to me. I can't offer you anything more than a night, but I believe it will be a night neither of us would forget."

Hadley nodded, but before she could firmly commit, there was a commotion on the dance floor. She looked up in time to see Weston and Piper moving out of the way of a falling beam. She clapped a hand to her mouth and gasped, moving away from Nykal as she instinctively went to check on the commander and Piper.

In the ensuing chaos, she lost track of Nykal, and by the time everything had returned to a semi-normal state, both Krill and Nykal were gone. If she wanted to see him again, her only option was to visit him in his quarters later that night.

In other words, she would have to sneak around and be his dirty little secret. The idea bothered her, but not as much as letting the opportunity to be with him slide into oblivion.

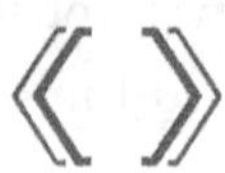

LONG AFTER THE RECEPTION, Hadley paced in her quarters as she gathered the courage to go to him. Only when she realized all her fears were of the consequences afterward, rather than from being with him, was she able to firm her shoulders and slip out of her quarters.

She'd changed into something more casual hours ago, but not so casual as to stand out. It wasn't like she was going to the prince in only a coat. If anyone saw her at this moment, they wouldn't think twice about her walking the station. What would raise eyebrows was if anyone saw her enter the prince's quarters. She had to be discreet.

She reached the guest quarters of the station a few minutes later. Krill was still in the room beside Nykal's, since he hadn't moved into his permanent quarters yet. They hadn't suited his preferences, so Weston had ordered a rush from Maintenance to put everything in order. The quarters wouldn't be available for a few days, until the renovations were finished. Hadley had overseen the room herself before their arrival, and Krill had seemed fine with it until he'd learned she was the one to prepare it. Then he'd found a million little things to nitpick, so the crew of the station had to redesign and rearrange.

With that in mind, she quietly tapped on Nykal's door. She didn't try to bypass the biometric panel security to gain entry. That would've been rude and improper, though she was fairly certain Nykal wouldn't have cared.

The door opened almost as soon as she rapped against it, and she slipped inside when he held out a hand. When the door closed behind her a moment later, she found herself in his arms. "I feel like a spy sneaking around."

"I apologize it has to be this way." He looked mournful. "I'd love for us to be far more open about a night together, but it would bring negative consequences to both of us."

She nodded, reaching up to smooth his furrowed orange brow. "It's okay. I totally understand, and one night together in secret is better than nothing, isn't it?"

"I sincerely believe that's true." With those words, Nykal bent his head, and Hadley lifted hers to meet him halfway. His lips molded to hers, and the kiss sent sparks from her lips all the way to her tiptoes. She tingled in spots she'd never recognized before, and her arms rose to clasp around his neck, holding him tighter to her. Hadley threaded her fingers in his hair, finding it just as silky as it looked, and anchored his mouth against hers.

Nykal seemed to have an innate grasp of how her garment functioned, and he found the hidden loop at the shoulder. Seconds later, the dress pooled at her feet, and she stepped out of it. She hadn't bothered with undergarments, so now she was nude before him.

His hands roamed over her body, caressing her curves and cupping one of her breasts. He moaned low in his throat, and she did the same when he tugged lightly on the nipple. She moaned again when he stepped back, breaking the embrace.

"Shush, I darling. I just want to look at you."

She opened her eyes, finding he had shed his robe as he stepped back. They were naked in front of each other, and his body was glorious. He definitely had a humanoid shape, complete with chiseled muscles and a narrow waist. She discovered the faint black striping was more visible under the places covered by clothing, and she reached out to stroke one of the stripes across his chest. "Why is it darker here?"

"There's not as much direct sunlight on those parts of our skin. Sunlight somewhat fades the black stripes."

He reached out, cradling both of her breasts. "This is different to me. Jroj females have four breasts instead of two."

She felt slightly awkward about that. "Sorry?"

Nykal laughed. "There's nothing to be sorry for. I like this way better. I have two hands, and you have two breasts. It works out quite nicely. Your breasts are taut and quite rounded. Much different from breasts I've seen in the past."

She took a step closer. "As much as I enjoy learning about your culture, don't take this the wrong way, but I really don't want to hear about breasts you've seen in the past."

He chuckled. "Fair enough."

She reached out, putting a hand around his shaft. He was thick and wide, with just the slightest dusting of fur. It was strange, but not off-putting. When her hand dipped lower, she was surprised to find no testicles. She hadn't delved that deeply into her research, and she made a mental note to look up physiology of Jroj men later. Much, much later.

"What do you like?" asked Nykal.

She moved closer, bending her head slightly to stroke her tongue across his nipple. "I'd like you to touch me."

"We should adjourn to my bedroom." He took her hand, leading her behind him.

Hadley happily went, and when the panel slid shut behind them, they approached the bed. He sat down, but then he looked surprised as she got on her knees in front of him. He frowned. "What are you doing?"

She licked her lips. "I'm tasting you."

Nykal looked confused. "I'm not sure I understand what you mean."

Her eyes widened. Perhaps Jrojans didn't do that. If he seemed to be offended, she would immediately withdraw, but the glistening drop of pre-cum at the tip of his cock beckoned her forward, and she flicked out her tongue to catch it. It tasted different from anything she'd had before. There was just the faintest hint of saltiness, and it had a fruitier floral taste than other partners she'd been with.

He let out a ragged gasp, and his hand went to her hair. He grabbed a handful of it, and she couldn't tell if he was trying to keep her from doing that again, or if he was trying to pull her closer.

"Have you never had this done to you before, Your Highness?" she teased.

Nykal let out a ragged gasp. "No, I haven't. I don't believe it's common among Jroj, though I'm not the best judge. I've only had a few encounters, and virtually none since Mygal's death."

She frowned. "You haven't had pleasure in ten solar cycles?"

He shrugged. "I've had self-pleasure, but that's not the same."

She shook her head. "Definitely not. I feel like I should make it up to you somehow." She spoke quietly as she dipped her head again, swirling her tongue around the head of his erection. His shaft was smooth and cylindrical, with a slight bulge farther down below what would be a human head.

She discovered when she wrapped her hand around the bulge and squeezed lightly that Nykal practically leapt off the bed as he arched his hips into the air and let out a sound somewhat like a purr. More than ever, he reminded her of a tiger at that moment, and she giggled before taking as much of his shaft into her mouth as she could. The bulge posed a unique challenge, since she was unable to fully encompass it with her mouth, so she continued to lightly massage it with her hand while sucking what she could get in her mouth.

Every time she ran her tongue over the tip of his shaft, he muttered and groaned while his body shook. He had incredible stamina, and her jaw was starting to hurt by the time his spasms were coming closer together. She genuinely wasn't certain what to expect, though she imagined there would be ejaculate just like with a human, since his pre-cum had increased the more she sucked him.

With a small cry, his hand in her hair tightened, and his hips lifted off the bed. His shaft tightened in her hand and mouth, and warm waves of his release filled her, spilling out of her lips. She swallowed as fast as could to keep it in, but some leaked out. He certainly produced a lot, and she wasn't certain if that was his normal biology, or if it was due to his deprivation over the last decade.

As he collapsed against the bed, she withdrew and discreetly wiped her mouth before moving to lie down beside him. She put her arm across his stomach and her head on his shoulder. "Have I killed you?"

He laughed softly. "If so, I've died happily. That was amazing, Hadley."

She lifted her head. "I guess your people have been missing out." She winked at him.

"I guess so." There was a slight growl in his tone, and his hand moved between her thighs. His fingers surged inside her liquid heat, and he growled again. "I would like to taste you now."

She moaned as he rubbed against her clit. "That's a bit rough there, tiger."

His eyes widened. "Have I hurt you?" His hand started to withdraw.

She immediately put hers atop his to keep him inside her. "No, you haven't hurt me, but my clitoris is tender." She positioned her finger over one of his, showing him the best way to stroke her clit. "It gives me incredible pleasure, but it's also very sensitive."

He nodded. "Like my knot."

"Is that the bulge in your shaft?" At his nod, she bit her lip. "And what does it do when you're having pleasure?"

He shrugged. "It intensifies it."

She marveled at the conversation they had. On one level, it seemed almost strictly educational, yet their fingers and hands were busy, lending an entirely new experience to what could have otherwise been an academic discussion.

"Will it harm you if I taste you there?" He wiggled his fingers inside her to emphasize which part he meant.

She shook her head. "Not as long as you don't get too rough."

Nykal slid down the bed until his knees were on the floor. He grasped her thighs and pulled her closer to the edge, and she let out a little squeal when his mouth immediately settled on her core. There was nothing tentative or shy about his touch. He dove right in, his tongue squirming into all the nooks and crannies of her slit. She moaned and whimpered under the onslaught of his tongue, finding that if he lacked experience, he certainly made up for it with enthusiasm.

He seemed fixated on her clit, at first trailing his tongue around it very lightly, but as he progressed, his confidence grew, and he applied more pressure. She hovered on the edge of orgasm in no time, and she clasped the cover on his bed in her fists, arching her hips upward when the flat side of his tongue pressed fully against her clitoral hood, sending her over the edge. She let out a cry and then another as the pleasure built. She tried to wriggle away from him, and he seemed to realize she needed a break at that point, because his tongue ceased. Pleasure consumed her, and she shook under the blitz. She'd never felt so ravished or so satisfied.

When the pleasure finally faded enough for her to think and speak again, she parted her thighs wider. "Do you know this part?"

He nodded. "This is the part the Jroj do as well." He stood up, lifting her into his arms. She tightened her thighs around his hips, and Nykal carried her to the other side of the bed, so they could lie down together. As they got into position, his shaft slipped inside her, and she moaned at the intrusion.

His generous size was decadent, if a little more than she was used to. His lightly furred cock added a new, interesting sensation she'd never experienced before, and his knot had the fortuitous benefit of resting just against her g-spot when he was fully inside her. Each thrust stimulated that sensitive area, and she clung to him with her thighs still wrapped around him, and her fingers digging into his back. She was afraid she was leaving scratches with her nails, but she couldn't control the animalistic impulses racing through her as he thrust in and out of her.

Her sheath spasmed around him moments later, and she came again with a keening cry. Seconds after, Nykal apparently decided to surrender his tenuous control, because his seed filled her. The knot in his cock swelled for a moment, leaving him wedged firmly inside her.

She wondered in an abstract way if they would be joined for a while, but almost immediately after he stopped coming, his shaft returned to normal size. He pulled out from her, and then rolled over with her against his side. He pressed a kiss to her temple and held her. "I've never experienced anything like that before. It's never been this way."

She mumbled something that was almost intelligible before clearing her throat and trying again. "Neither have I." Sex with others had never been this amazing or memorable. Perhaps a touch of it was the exoticness of his biology, and the differences in their cultural ways of lovemaking, but most of it was just him. She had no doubt about that. Even if they'd had boring missionary sex with nothing else, she couldn't believe it wouldn't have been the most amazing sex of her life.

They spent the rest of the night dozing in between making love. She was sore and sated by early morning. They stood near his door, and he gave her one last long, drugging kiss. It was almost impossible to let go of him, but she finally forced herself to take a step back. "Tonight's meant so much to me, Nykal."

He smiled, but there was sadness in his eyes. "It's the same for me, Hadley. I'm never going to forget you."

She nodded. "I'll never forget you either." She sniffled when tears threatened, managing to stifle them all except for one teardrop that trailed down her cheek slowly.

He wiped it away. "I didn't mean to make you sad."

She smiled. "I did the same to you. We both knew the end would be awful, didn't we? And yet, I don't doubt at all that the pleasure we shared is worth this pain now."

"I concur." He bent down once more, pressing a kiss to her forehead instead of her lips. "Be well and take care of yourself, Hadley."

"I will, and you too, Your Highness. I hope you find happiness in the role that's been thrust upon you." She kissed his cheek, denying herself the temptation of his lips, or she might never be able to walk away. A moment later, he pressed his hand to the biometric panel, and the door slid open behind her.

She darted out and turned away, forcing herself to keep walking without looking back. There was no doubt at all this was a goodbye, and for a moment she regretted giving in to temptation.

How was she supposed to keep going after discovering how it could be with him? But she couldn't hold on to him, and he couldn't stay. One night of bliss would have to be enough for both of them. One thing was certain. She would never forget Nykal for as long as she lived. She hoped it was true when he'd said the same to her. She had no reason to doubt his sincerity.

She supposed she should hope he'd soon move on from her and find someone else to make him happy. It would be better for both if they could quickly forget each other. Hadley knew it wouldn't be that simple for her. She must not be that altruistic, because part of her liked the idea of leaving an indelible imprint on him that assured he would never forget her either.

Chapter Three

THE NEXT FEW WEEKS were miserable, though Hadley did her best to hide how she felt. She couldn't stop thinking about the prince during her free moments. More than once, she was tempted to send him a message, but common sense won out. It was likely all his messages would've been intercepted by aides, since she didn't have his direct communication code. Many would question why the second-in-command of Olympus Station was sending the prince personal missives, and it would just lead to scandal and problems for both of them.

Her lack of sleep must be catching up with her, because she was worn out and exhausted. She would've gone to see Gretel, but she knew what was wrong with her—heartbreak 'flu. It was a physical manifestation of how sad she was, and how little sleep she'd gotten.

At least that was what she thought until she was on the promenade that housed the open-air markets, and she passed a purple woman with yellow hair. She jumped with surprise when Abira put a hand on her arm. "Do you need something, Abira?"

The alien woman smiled at her. "It's not me who needs. It's you." She thrust out a charm. When she spun it, the thing made a shrill whistling sound.

Hadley winced as she stared at it with alarm, instantly recognizing it as one of the charms Abira gave to expectant mothers. In her culture, it was meant to protect against to miscarriage and ensure a pain-free delivery. "I don't need that." There was a sharp edged her tone when she refused to accept it.

"It's good luck for you and the child." She thrust it more insistently, shaking it.

"I really don't…" She trailed off as she realized people were starting to stare as they passed. She quickly snatched the charm from Abira and nodded her head. "Thank you."

"Wear it touching your belly." Abira selected a long piece of cord that looked like real leather. She took the charm from Hadley again and tied it to the cord before handing it to her and gesturing for her to put it around her neck.

Hadley was eager to escape, so she did so quickly, even overcoming her distaste at wearing animal skin. The charm rested right against her belly. It must be her imagination, but she felt warmth where it touched. "Thanks."

"Of course, Captain Wells." Abira nodded to her with a knowing look before turning to offer another customer coming by a different item entirely.

As soon as Hadley was out of sight, she took off the charm and stuffed it in her pocket. She was concerned, because Abira seemed to know exactly when various species around the station were expecting children. As far as Hadley knew, she'd never been wrong.

She'd just gotten off-shift, and her plan had been to go back to her quarters to try to catch up on sleep, but now she detoured to Medical. The last thing she wanted to do was face the possibility she might be pregnant by Nykal, but putting it off wouldn't help the situation. The sooner she knew, the sooner she could formulate a plan.

She was relieved to find no one waiting in medical, and Gretel was leaned back with a datapad on her lap, sipping something green from a clear cup. "I'm surprised you're still here this late," said Hadley as the door closed behind her.

Gretel looked up and smiled. "Hadley, how are you? I'm just filling in for someone else who's ill. I don't usually work the later shift."

"Is there somewhere we can talk more privately?"

Gretel's eyes widened. "I take it you're here for personal rather than station business?" At Hadley's nod, she gestured her forward toward an exam room. Gretel entered first, and Hadley followed her. She was pleased when Gretel sealed the door with her palm, so no one else could enter.

"What brings you here, Captain?"

Without speaking, Hadley reached into her pocket and pulled out the charm Abira had given her. She opened her palm to show it to Gretel, who looked surprised, and then worried.

"You didn't just find that in the corridor, did you?" asked Gretel with an air of hope.

Hadley snorted. "I wish. Abira practically forced me to accept it."

"And is there a possibility you could be expecting?"

Hadley frowned. "I truly don't see how. I have a Biochip, but I have had sex recently."

"We'd best test, but I think we should do so discreetly?" At Hadley's nod, she created an anonymous file. "There you are. You're a number in the system for now, and if it turns out positive, you can apply for a backdated permit from the Reproduction Board with this number. At some point, you'll have to reveal your name and profession, but this will buy you some time to deal with any difficulties."

"You don't know the half of it," said Hadley. A surge of nausea burned in her throat, but she wasn't certain if that was nerves or the onset of morning sickness. Surely it couldn't be that. Abira had to be wrong.

Gretel had her lie down on the table and ran the scanner across her body. She paused over her stomach, and the screen above showed a little blobby thing that was definitely moving. "Is that a baby?" asked Hadley, feeling ill again.

Gretel frowned. "I'm afraid so. You appear about eight weeks along."

Panic seized her. "That can't be. There's only one possible date of conception, and that was three weeks ago."

"Hmm. What is the species of the father?"

She was reluctant, but had to give Gretel all the information. "Jroj."

Gretel paused, looking stunned before her professional expression returned. "Not Krill, I take it?"

She snorted. "Not hardly."

Gretel sighed. "That's certainly a complication. Let me do some digging here..." She trailed off as she tapped on her datapad. Pages of documents replaced the scan on the screen, and she nodded after a couple of minutes. She scrolled through, muttering tidbits as she went.

"They have a bulge on their penis... I bet you knew that." More scrolling. "Ah, it holds the sperm and swells at ejaculation to ensure adequate time for conception. Interesting..." Then she stopped and focused for a moment. "Ah ha."

"What?" asked Hadley, preparing herself for something awful.

"The gestational rate for Jroj is less than human, but I doubt it would be quite as quick since your fetus has human DNA too. I'm just guessing that you'll be due in about six months, based on the differences in growth size for what we'd expect with a human fetus and what you're carrying. I have to monitor closely to check growth though, because you're the first. There aren't any documented human-Jroj pregnancies in Coalition databanks. I have no idea what to expect exactly, so I want to see you every week."

Hadley groaned. "How did this happen? Did my Biochip malfunction?"

Gretel didn't answer, but the scanner repositioned to focus on her head. A picture of her brain appeared on the screen, replacing the documents, and Gretel zoomed in on one area that had a small white rectangle embedded in it. "I'm performing the diagnostic now. Just a second... No, it's functioning normally."

"It can't be, or I wouldn't be pregnant. How did this happen?" Hadley could see her career crumbling before her eyes. If word got out that the father of her child was the prince of a race that recently joined the Coalition, the fallout would be awful. Not only would she lose her job, but she'd probably lose her pension and ranking. She could also forget easily finding a civilian job with that mark on her record.

Even worse, what if she was denied a permit to reproduce? She'd either have to leave Coalition territory or accept an abortion.

Her heart cried out in refusal of that idea, and before she really entertained the thought, she already knew her answer if Gretel asked. There was no way she was going to terminate this pregnancy. It was the tiniest piece of the prince, and she intended to cling to it. It was her too, and though their child had been conceived accidentally, that didn't mean she didn't want it.

"This is my best guess, but after looking through the database, the Biochip doesn't have a profile for Jroj sperm in storage. Likely, the Biochip didn't recognize it as something that risked making you pregnant, so it didn't destroy the sperm. It slipped right through without recognition."

"How did that happen?"

"Not everything's been added to the Coalition database yet. You know how long these things can take. We're talking about adding an entire culture to our memory databanks. There's language, biology, customs, etc. It takes months to solar cycles to get everything caught up when we have a group newly joining the Coalition."

"Maybe you should suggest they update the sperm profiles sooner rather than later?" She groaned. "I can't believe this is happening."

"You're early enough along that there are other options."

She firmed her lips. "No abortion."

Gretel didn't blink. "Okay. There are still other possibilities that don't require termination, if you don't want to carry the pregnancy yourself. You could remove and freeze the fetus, which has an eighty percent survival rate upon reimplantation. Or you could find a donor uterus, especially if you have a close family member. You have a sister, don't you?"

Hadley nodded. "I do, but I couldn't ask her to do that. She has three children of her own and lives on a farming colony with her husband. She's run ragged, and she wouldn't want to raise my child." Hadley couldn't bear the thought of letting go of the baby anyway. "I'm not going to do anything besides let it run its course." She touched her stomach. "I want this baby. I certainly didn't plan it, and I don't know how I'm going to make it work, but I can't imagine removing it from my body for any reason."

Gretel's expression softened. "In that case, congratulations, and I'll do my best to help you keep it discreet as long as we can."

Hadley squeezed Gretel's hands. "You're a good friend. Thank you."

"I'll see if I can expedite your permit. I have a few contacts at the Coalition Reproductive Board, and after Baxter Frink tried to kill Piper, I figure they owe us a few. Right?" She grinned.

Hadley nodded, though she wasn't quite able to muster a smile. She was excited about having Nykal's baby, but she was terrified too. It would change so many things, and she had no idea how she was going to proceed. Right now, the paramount thing was keeping the pregnancy hidden while she decided how she was going to handle the future.

AS SHE WAS LEAVING Medical a short time later, she literally almost ran into Ambassador Krill. "Oh, excuse me, Ambassador. I wasn't paying attention to where I was going, I guess." In actuality, it seemed like the ambassador had been the one who almost plowed into her, but she knew to take the blame, especially with this guy.

He glared at her. "The prince is coming for a surprise visit."

She struggled to keep any reaction from her face. "Oh, I hope there's no emergency at home?"

"There's no emergency, and no good reason for him to return to Olympus Station. No good reason at all." His gaze raked over her dismissively. "Did you review the etiquette protocols you were given before our arrival, Captain Wells?"

She frowned. "Of course I did, Ambassador Krill. I'm good at my job."

He sniffed. "Do you remember the part that forbids mingling Jroj DNA with any other outside race?"

She stiffened as fear shot through her. How could he possibly know she was pregnant? Thankfully, before she could blurt out something that revealed her secret, he continued.

"That implicitly prevents Jroj from dating outside our species as well. We're a race of isolationists, though some of the younger ones want to make us open to the outside. The prince and others can force us to open economically, but they can't change thousands of solar cycles of entrenched culture. Jroj marry Jroj, and affairs outside of our race won't be tolerated. "

"Why are you telling me this, Ambassador? Has someone here on the station caught your eye?" She asked the question sweetly, not admitting to anything.

He sneered. "None of these inferior races could ever catch my eye. You would do well to remember the restrictions in place on the prince, and I intend to remind him as well."

"It sounds like you're as good at your job as I am at mine. If you'll excuse me, there are things I need to tend to?" She walked away with her head held high and her shoulders squared, refusing to admit anything, even through body language.

Inside, she was a quaking mass of fear, but relieved he clearly hadn't figured out she was pregnant. He was just warning her off an affair with the prince. How much did he know versus how much did he suspect? Had he seen her leave Nykal's room three weeks ago? If so, he hadn't said anything until now, which made sense. Nykal was returning for an unexpected visit, and Hadley was sure she was the real reason. Unfortunately, Krill had figured that out as well and realized their affair hadn't been a one-time thing—or suspected that. They would have to be careful and more discreet.

She still didn't know if she should tell Nykal about the baby. It didn't seem like the right thing to do with so many barriers between them, but she hated the thought of hiding their child from him as well. That felt wrong on so many levels. She had no idea what she was going to do, but she couldn't deny she was excited about the possibility of seeing Nykal again.

Chapter Four

NYKAL STEPPED OFF THE transport ship, trying to hide a grimace at the sight of Krill waiting for him. Clearly, the other man was annoyed, and his frill had risen halfway. Nykal struggled for a polite smile as he reached the ambassador. He bent his head in a respectful fashion, though of course he wasn't required to do that due to his rank. "It's unexpected to see you waiting for me, Ambassador. I thought we had scheduled dinner for later?"

The ambassador sniffed at him. "I find myself occupied with important matters of state, so we won't be able to meet to share nourishment."

He struggled to hide his pleasure at the knowledge. "That's unfortunate."

"Perhaps unfettered access to what brought you here will get it out of your system, so you can resume your proper duties." With those veiled words, Krill turned and marched away without a parting.

As the Crown Prince, he could have taken issue with Krill's admonishment and behavior, but he was just glad not to have to deal with the man during his brief visit. He wondered how much Krill had guessed, and he assumed quite a bit about his true motives for arriving at Olympus Station. He'd left Palos with little notice, having given in to the urge to return to the station to see Hadley again.

His aides and advisers had protested, but Vasar had been happy to step in for him when he supposedly came to handle an issue that was simply a pretext to get him there. Nykal wondered if others had guessed, and he was concerned about dragging Hadley into a scandal, but he couldn't deny the need to see her again. One taste of her made him want another, and he'd spent the last three weeks dreaming of her and thinking about her when he was awake. He'd tried to rack his brain to think of a way they could be together, but he'd found no solution so far.

For all he knew, she might not want anything more than an occasional night like the one they'd shared before. He didn't want to rush her or be too forward, but if she would agree to come back with him to Jroj, he'd find a way to make it happen.

He spent the next hour searching the station for her. He tried asking the A.I. program at one of the kiosks to locate her, but since he wasn't a resident with official business, the computer denied him the knowledge. If she was on the command deck, he couldn't go there without a good reason, so he ended up making his way to the area labeled as Crew Quarters on the kiosk's map.

Of course, access required a biometric scan that he couldn't provide, so he had to wait near the doors as crew came and went. His only hope was Hadley would come by at some point and see him. He had nightmares of having to spend all his time allotted for the entire trip parked against the wall where he now sat, waiting for her to come.

At least he'd come incognito, as much as he could. He wore a black robe with a hood, and he had deliberately declined security, though his guards had been unhappy. His crown was safely in his quarters on the ship, and there was little to give away his identity unless someone already knew who he was.

He leaned his head back against the wall, planning just to relax and keep an eye open for her, but as the time stretched, his eyelids started to close. He blinked, trying to wake himself up, but ended up dozing off.

He knew he must have, because the next time he woke, it was to the sharp jab of something against his shoulder. With a groan, he opened his eyes and stared up at two people wearing security uniforms for

Olympus Station. He muttered a groan again. The situation had just gotten worse.

"You can't to sleep here, buddy. If you need quarters, there are temporary ones available for a reasonable fee." That came from the gruff older man.

"There's also an assistance program you can apply for if you need funds to stay on Olympus Station. You can stay up to four weeks without declaring an official purpose." The female security officer seemed slightly kinder, but she was still firm when she said, "You can't camp out wherever you want though."

He grimaced. "I'm waiting for someone."

The guards traded a glance, clearly disbelieving. "Oh, yeah? Who's that?" asked the older man.

"Hadley... Wells." He tacked on her last name to add authenticity.

The elder guard snorted. "Sure you are. Get up, and we'll escort you to the temporary quarters."

He pushed back the hood as he got to his feet, which put him about six inches taller than the older man. "I'm not going anywhere until I see Hadley. I'm not a transient, and I don't need temporary housing. I just need to see Captain Wells."

"Then you should've made an appointment to see her at her office," said the younger woman. "You can't stay here. Let's go."

He heaved a sigh. "If I go with you to where it is you want, are you going to contact Hadley to let her know I'm here?"

"No." The other man prodded him lightly with the butt of his rifle. "Now get going."

He drew himself to his full height. He didn't bother with looking at the older man, since he'd already labeled him as unreasonable. Instead, he focused his attention on the younger guard. "My name is Nykal Atole, and I'm the Crown Prince of Jroj. I know Captain Wells and Commander Templeton from a recent visit. Ambassador Krill can also vouch for my identity.

"I suggest you contact one of them before you create a diplomatic incident that has far-reaching consequences for your career. I don't believe the Coalition will take kindly to arresting the future ruler of one of its member planets." He hated pulling the imperious prince routine, but he wasn't about to let these two arrest him for however long before they were satisfied, and lose precious time with Hadley. "I'd prefer you contact Captain Wells."

"Not a chance in hell," said the man.

Thanks to Hadley, he recognized that word and scowled at the uncooperative guard.

The woman looked a little anxious. "I think maybe we should, Hayes."

The one now identified as Hayes snorted. "Are you really that gullible, Ipsy? Does he look like a prince to you?"

Nykal realized his choice of garb might count against him now, since he'd deliberately cultivated a nondescript appearance. He looked at Ipsy. "I'm dressing discreetly so as not to cause a stir. If you'd like to scan your databanks, I'm certain you'll find a match for me. I was a visitor here recently, after all."

She looked down at her comm, and her eyes widened slightly after a minute. "His name is in the system, Hayes."

Hayes shook his head. "Fine, let yourself get conned. It's all on you, Ipsy."

She looked hesitant for a moment, and then she touched a button on her wrist comm. "A.I., find Captain Wells."

Nykal sagged lightly against the wall when Hadley's voice came through the woman's wrist comm. "This is Captain Hadley Wells. How may I help you?"

"Good afternoon, ma'am. This is Security Agent Emily Ipsy. You have a visitor. Well, he claims he's your visitor. Do you know Prince Nykal Atole?"

He couldn't see her, but he could clearly hear her gasp of shock. "Yes, of course I do." There was a pause. "Where is he?"

"He's camped out near the crew quarters," said Hayes over Ipsy's shoulder. "This guy looks like a space bum."

Nykal laughed at the hyperbole. He'd dressed down, but he certainly didn't look like a vagrant.

"I see. In that case... Show him to my quarters, please. Use security override Sigma Alpha Two to grant him admission. Thank you for calling me."

"Thank you, Captain Wells." Ipsy ended the connection a moment later, and she looked embarrassed when she glanced at Nykal again. "I'm sorry for the misunderstanding, Your Highness."

Hayes looked moderately uncomfortable now that he realized he'd behaved badly, and it could come back to haunt him. Nykal wasn't inclined to hold a grudge, especially since he would see Hadley soon. He just ignored the other man as he nodded at Ipsy. "It's fine. Could you please show me to her quarters now?"

"Of course, Your Highness." With an obsequious bow, she moved ahead of him, and Nykal fell into step behind her. He was aware of Hayes bringing up the rear, and he suspected the other man still held his laser rifle at the ready, as though he would shoot Nykal at the first sign of any issue. He was mostly amused, but slightly unnerved. It was a relief to reach Hadley's quarters two minutes later. He stood by while Ipsy implemented Override Sigma Alpha Two, and her door opened a millisecond later with a hydraulic hiss.

He crossed into the quarters and nodded at Ipsy. "Thank you again for your assistance."

She bent once more in a bow, nodding all the while. "Of course, Your Highness. Once more, I'm sorry for the mix-up."

He waved a hand. "It's no longer a concern." Then he closed the door on both of them without acknowledging Hayes again. He doubted Hayes would care to be denied a word of parting from him.

He paced her quarters, soon realizing she wasn't coming right away. He went to the synthicator and created himself a meal while he waited for her. He thought about creating one for her as well, but she'd probably rather have it warm. He also didn't know her preferences. They were just one of the long list of things he longed to know about her. He could learn basics like that from her Favorites list on the synthicator, but he'd rather learn them from her lips directly.

As the evening passed, he started to fear he wouldn't have much time with her at all. He ordered a Denariian wine and curled up on the couch to wait for her. It seemed like no time at all had passed, and then he realized why. He must've dozed off, and now he woke at the sound of her entry. A glance at the solar clock projected on the wall revealed he'd been waiting for her almost three hours.

She approached him wearing her gray uniform and a frown. "What are you doing here?"

He was put off by her tone. "I wanted to see you. I managed to squeeze in a quick visit. I hope that's okay?"

She nodded jerkily. "It's fine, but if I'd known, I could've rearranged my schedule a bit. My only notice was a veiled warning from Krill, without specifics."

He frowned. "Krill approached you."

She sighed wearily. "Yep. And I thought you'd comm or something if you actually showed up. I couldn't rearrange my schedule without notice." She sighed again. "I just got off-shift." She looked exhausted.

He sat up. "May I synthicate you a meal?"

She let out a long sigh as she reached up to undo her hair. "Please. I'm going to change to something more comfortable. Oh, but no hummus of any sort. I just can't handle it right now." After she said that, she looked worried for a moment before rushing to her room.

He was confused by her reaction, and by the distance in her greeting. He'd expected her to at least hug or kiss him before she went to change, and he started to wonder if he'd made a mistake in coming.

He went to the synthicator and examined the list of her favorite meals, picking the one at the top. The food appeared an instant later, and he carried it to the table. He added a glass of Denariian wine as well, since he'd enjoyed it so much.

When she came out, she went straight to the table and sat down, still separating from him. She leaned back, making it easy to see the lines of exhaustion etched in her face, and he wondered if she was having as much trouble sleeping as he was.

She reached for her fork, seeming to ignore the wine entirely. After her first bite, she closed her eyes with a moan of pleasure. "I'm starving. I didn't get a chance to synthicate nourishment during my shift, and I can't seem to get full some days." She shook her head, eyes wide. "Never mind. So why are you here?"

"I had to see you again. I've spent the last three weeks thinking about you, and it became an urgent need. I apologize if it's not reciprocated."

Her expression softened, and she reached over to touch his hand. "It's very much reciprocated. I guess I'm just tired, and I didn't know if you were really coming. I didn't mean for you to have to wait so long to see me."

He felt much better with just a simple touch, and he smiled. "I don't mind waiting. I feel like I'd wait forever for you, Hadley." She looked like she was going to cry, and she blinked rapidly. He was alarmed by the thought, certain he'd said something wrong. "Whatever I did, I'm sorry."

She laughed, though the sound was a little watery, and resumed eating. "You didn't do anything. I'm just happy to see you. I shouldn't be, since I know we can't keep doing this, but I'm so glad you were able to find a way to come see me."

"I couldn't stay away."

While they talked during the meal, she slowly relaxed. He wasn't certain why she was so tense, but obviously something weighed on her mind. Without her being inclined to share, he couldn't force her to, so he just tried to draw her out of her melancholy, trying anything to get her smiling and laughing again.

After her dinner, they moved to her room. He spent the next two hours thoroughly making love to her. During his time apart from her, Nykal had spent some time researching various human sexual practices, and he'd added to his repertoire this time around. He left her breathless and quaking, and they later collapsed into a puddle of pleasure on the bed. Then he gathered her in his arms and slept better than he had in weeks.

SHE WAS STILL FIRMLY in his arms when he woke early the next morning. The chirp of the alarm she'd set before they fell asleep woke him, and he was concerned about her having to go back to work on so little sleep. He needed to leave soon to return to the palace in the capitol city of Palos, but he wished she could sleep longer.

She sat up and stretched as she yawned. She looked much better than she had when he'd first seen her last night. She smiled at him. "I'd like to offer you breakfast in bed, but I literally have no time. I pushed the alarm out as far as I dare without being late."

He swallowed his disappointment that their time together had come to an end again. Considering he'd never expected to have a second night with her, he should be grateful they'd had even the last few hours, but it was difficult to feel gratitude when parting from her again was imminent. He took her hand and brought it to his mouth, kissing her fingertips. Her eyes closed, and she moaned softly at the sensual touch. "I'm thankful for the time we had."

She nodded, her eyes slowly opening. "I didn't expect to see you again."

Impulsively, he said, "I want you to come with me to Jroj."

She frowned. "For a visit?"

He nodded. "I'd love to show you my planet. It's not as lovely as the Senufo planet you showed me on the VR platform, but it's quite breathtaking in places. We could spend a few weeks exploring it."

Her expression closed. "I don't have a few weeks." She swallowed audibly. "I mean I have to work, so I can't do that. Thank you for the invitation though. Maybe when I have vacation time coming, I can visit you?"

Her words stung, because they felt like a dismissal. He frowned. "Have I misinterpreted something?"

She arched a brow. "What do you mean?"

"You seem almost unhappy that I came to visit."

She shook her head, and her expression was soft. "I'm thrilled you came to visit. It's going to make it harder to say goodbye again, but I did enjoy seeing you. I just know this can't continue."

Nykal took her hand in his, clutching tightly. "Maybe we can find a way to make it work."

Her lower lip wobbled, and she didn't seem like she believed him, though she nodded. "Maybe. If you can next time, make sure you give me notice so I can have more time to be with you."

He nodded at the stipulation. "I wish I didn't have to leave, or you were coming with me."

"It would be nice if you could stay with me." She sighed heavily. "I really have to get ready for work. I'm sorry we don't have more time together."

He understood that was the cue for him to get ready to leave, so he stood up and dressed. She walked him to the door, and they shared one last lingering kiss before she opened it, and he slipped into the corridor. He followed the corridors to the exit, joining a small line of people who were entering the station lift from the crew quarters. No one gave him a second look, so there was no need to explain why he was there.

The farther he got from her, the more physically painful it was to be parted. By the time he reached his shuttle, it took all his determination to board the craft and not run back to find her. He suspected he was in the early stages of *viiraria*, which was the bonding process between mates on his planet.

It was physically painful to be parted from one's mate and denied exposure to their pheromones and presence. That faded over time as the partners adjusted to each other, but he knew the bond would strengthen in intensity if he continued to see her. He should tell her what he was feeling, and what it represented. Either that, or he should make the decision to stay away before the *viiraria* could fully develop and cause problems neither one of them were ready to face.

Chapter Five

HADLEY'S MORNING STARTED on the right foot, though it was hard to watch Nykal leave. She was grateful for the night they'd had together, but she still felt bad that she hadn't told him about the baby. She wasn't sure how she could, or what she could say. How could they make it work? He was probably unable to officially acknowledge the child, so would a discreet relationship with his child via intermittent visits be better than him or the baby never knowing about each other? She didn't have an answer for that, which weighed on her.

It wasn't enough to stifle her good mood, especially since she'd woken without nausea. That had plagued her the last few mornings, but not today.

She set about her morning duties, managing to find a hint of optimism that perhaps things weren't completely impossible with Nykal. It was obvious he wanted to be with her, though she still didn't know how much. Was it the equivalent of an alien booty call for him, or was there more to it? She knew for her, there was certainly more developing. She was rapidly falling for the Jrojan prince, which alarmed her, but not enough to stop her from feeling that way.

The call from Ambassador Krill at midday interrupted what was otherwise a fair day for her, despite her doubts and fears. She headed to his office, hoping he was complaining about the facilities again, though she suspected it might be a more personal matter. That thought filled her with dread, and she experienced the first surge of nausea all day.

She wasn't at all surprised to see he had a Jroj receptionist, since he didn't seem like the kind who would hire outside his species. The young man gave her a severe frown and examined the appointment book with great care as he loaded it onto the screen, as though he suspected she was trying to get past him to assassinate Krill. If only.

After a long moment of study, he nodded. "You may go in, Captain Wells."

"Thanks." She rushed past him to the inner office, knocking on the door as she entered to give Krill a heads-up of her arrival.

He sat at his desk, not bothering to rise to meet her. "Close the door behind you."

She did so, using her palm to seal it. She was more certain than ever that whatever he had to say to her, she didn't want others to hear, and it probably had nothing to do with the ten cubic centimeters of which he felt cheated.

She approached the desk, standing stiffly in front of it. He didn't invite her to sit down, and she didn't presume to. She didn't want to get comfortable and linger anyway. "What can I do for you today, Ambassador Krill?"

He stared up at her with his dark, inscrutable eyes, though his expression revealed his distaste. "I can't imagine what he sees in you."

She stiffened at the insult. "And I'm sure it's not your business." He slammed his hand on the desk, which made Hadley jump despite her best intentions not to show any reaction.

"It's my business when it affects my planet. I trust he's gotten you out of his system now, but if he tries to see you again, you're to tell him no."

She drew herself to her full height, scowling down at him. "I'll do as I wish, Ambassador Krill. You have no sway over me."

He gave a cold smile that sent a chill down her spine. "Perhaps not with you, but I do with the Coalition. I imagine the right word in the right ear would make it easy enough to sabotage your career."

She swallowed the lump in her throat, refusing to show any hint of being intimidated. "It isn't your business what happens between myself and him." She was careful not to mention Nykal's name. She doubted they were being recorded in any fashion, but without being sure, she wanted to be discreet.

"Let me put it more bluntly for you then. Perhaps I couldn't influence your career in a negative fashion, but you're breaking Jroj law by sleeping with him. If it continues, I'll petition to have you extradited, and you'll be charged with crimes against the Crown. You'll automatically be executed upon your conviction, and I promise you will be convicted.

Hadley's mouth dropped open. "You're threatening to have me killed?"

He shrugged. "Let's call it a promise, not a threat."

She trembled on the inside, but kept her expression stoic. "Is that all, Ambassador Krill?"

His deeply unpleasant smile managed to find another level of revolting. "Did you know the prince is betrothed?"

She stiffened at the news, both because he'd mentioned the prince, and because of the unwelcome fact. "I don't believe you."

With a sly chuckle, Krill pressed a button on his datapad. An image filled the screen on the wall a moment later, and it was of Nykal standing stiffly beside a Jrojan woman wearing what looked like a spun gold gown. She had a diadem on her head, and there was something regal about her.

"The woman standing beside him is Lady Layala Drestin. She's been trained from birth for a royal match and comes from a long line of suitable nobles. She will be an enhancement to his power and far more than just a pretty adornment. Their children will both be Jroj. Lady Layala has been raised with proper breeding and decorum. In short, she's everything you're not, and she's the one who will marry Prince Nykal."

Hadley struggled to take a deep breath, wanting to deny what she was seeing. She refused to let the tears pricking the back of her eyes fall or give Krill further satisfaction. Without looking at him, she asked, "Is there anything else I can do for you as second-in-command of Olympus Station, Ambassador Krill?"

"Do as you're asked, and all will be fine. You're dismissed."

She didn't say another word to him as she turned and walked out of the office. She wandered in a daze for a few minutes after she left the section that housed the ambassadors' offices. She found herself on the lift and got out on the promenade level, though it hadn't been her intended destination.

She wasn't sure where she was headed, or what she was doing. That applied to far more than her immediate destination. She was entangled with an alien prince, and he had a waiting fiancée. Of course, he hadn't bothered to mention that when he was sleeping with her, and now she was pregnant. It was absolutely impossible to tell him about the baby now. She refused to have her child raised as a bastard, unacknowledged child of the prince.

Plus, there was the very real fear that Krill would order her death if he found out she was expecting Nykal's child. All he had to do was have her extradited to his planet to face execution, where she doubted they would give even a pretext of a fair trial. What was the point anyway, when she certainly couldn't deny she'd been involved with him? The proof was in her womb.

How was she going to do this? If she stayed on the station and gave birth to the child here, Krill might eventually see her baby and realize he had Jrojan DNA. It wouldn't be a far leap for him to assume Nykal was the father, and then she and her baby might both be at risk.

But the idea of leaving Olympus Station, which was her home, cut through her. She couldn't bear the thought either. She'd worked so hard to get where she was, and she loved her life here. Perhaps it wasn't the best place to raise a child, but there were childcare facilities and people she trusted here.

It was as safe as any other place in the galaxy, and if she asked to be reassigned, there was no telling where she might end up. She could list a preference, but there was no guarantee she'd actually get that assignment. She could end up at the ass-end of the galaxy on some place like Greer, where her friend Piper had been an exobotanist salvaging rare plants. Piper had enjoyed that, but she wouldn't. Even worse, she could end up in one of the rougher colonies that mined precious metals, where violence was common. She couldn't imagine raising her child that way.

She had no idea what she was going to do when she literally ran into Piper a few minutes later. Piper was emerging from one of the shops, and they collided. "I'm so sorry."

Piper shrugged a shoulder. She looked so much better after recovering from her experience with Baxter Frink. "It's all right. I'm glad to see you."

She managed to smile. "I'm happy to see you too. You look much better. Have you recovered?"

Piper nodded. "There wasn't a whole lot to recover from, other than some bruises on my throat. I was lucky enough not to see him jump to his death."

Hadley's lips wobbled suddenly. "That's good." Her voice was thick with tears.

Piper frowned. "What's the matter?"

Hadley waved a hand. "Nothing. I really have to go."

Instead of listening, Piper put her arm through Hadley's and drew her toward the bar. "Not without talking to me and telling me what's going on."

Hadley could have resisted, but she didn't really want to. What she'd just learned devastated her, and she wanted to talk. Yet she couldn't imagine taking Piper fully into her confidence, since Piper was about to be married to the commander of the station, and Weston was her boss. If he got wind of her unauthorized pregnancy, which had yet to receive a backdated permit, or even worse, learned who'd fathered her child, that could be the destruction of her career.

Piper steered them toward the back corner of the bar, and Anthracite, the head bartender, approached their table himself. He scowled at Piper, but asked, "Florfial firewheel?"

"If you hold the horg root," she said tartly with a nod.

Anthracite's expression softened slightly for Hadley, who'd known him for solar cycles. "Your usual Sinuvosh ale?"

She started to say yes, but then remembered why she shouldn't drink. Instead, she cleared her throat. "I'll be going on duty soon, so perhaps one of those firewheels for me too."

Anthracite looked surprised, but nodded before moving away. Hadley had been known to have a small tipple shortly before her shift every now and then, so he was probably surprised by her sudden need to be a stickler for rules.

"Tell me what's wrong."

Before answering Piper, she looked around. There were a few other patrons in the bar, but they were all on the other side of the room, so they had the space to themselves. She leaned forward, whispering her confession. Over the next few minutes, she told Piper about how she and the prince had started an affair that was technically illegal.

She paused only long enough for Anthracite to deliver their drinks, not wanting him to overhear a word, before resuming. The only thing she held back was the knowledge of her pregnancy. She couldn't admit that yet, especially not to Piper, who might tell Weston. With her upcoming wedding to Weston, it would be only natural for her to tell him everything. Hadley wouldn't even consider that a betrayal of confidence, because she knew they were close, and it would've weighed heavily on Piper not to tell Weston.

"There must be some way to be together." Piper sipped her firewheel.

Hadley shook her head. "Not that I can see. And with Krill's threat hanging over my head..." She shrugged. "Besides, didn't you hear the part where he's betrothed?"

Piper's expression turned angry. "Yes, and I think that's completely low of him not to tell you. But maybe he wants you more. I mean, they aren't married yet, right?"

Hadley shook her head. "It doesn't sound like it."

"There's still time to change his mind then."

Hadley snorted. "Do you think Weston would change his mind about marrying you?"

Piper scowled. "Of course not." Then her eyes sparkled. "I see what you're doing there, but I think the difference is I definitely love Weston, and he loves me. We don't know how the prince feels about this Lady Layala. He might loathe her."

"We don't usually marry people we loathe." Defeatism overtook her, and she set down the drink before she took a sip. "Really, it's hopeless. I just need to accept that. Our couple of nights together were all we're going to have. If I saw him again, I'd want to punch him anyway. He lied to me about being engaged. Well, he didn't lie exactly. He just never bothered to mention he was about to marry someone else. That's a pretty big lie by omission, don't you think?"

Piper nodded. "I'll agree with you there. It sounds like you'd be better off without him. We should have a girls' day. We could get massages and shop, or maybe get our fingers and toes done." She looked down at her belly. "I'm almost at the point where I swear I can't see my toes, though I'm only about twenty weeks along."

Hadley laughed. "It sounds like fun, but I don't think I'm up for it today. Maybe in a couple of days, when everything calms down." And when the nausea churning in her stomach settled again. She still hoped for a respite from the unrelenting nausea that had overtaken her the last couple of days. The likelihood didn't seem promising, since she felt on the verge of vomiting. On the other hand, she was still processing Krill's threat and the fact Nykal was engaged to someone else. No wonder her stomach refused to relax.

"In that case, I'm going to hold you to it. It could be good for you, and I could use some pampering too."

"Thank you, Piper. You're a good friend." She noticed Piper's drink was finished, though she'd barely touched her own. "I should probably get going."

Piper nodded. "Me too. Weston will be off-shift soon, and I'd like to synthicate dinner to have it waiting for him."

Hadley winked. "So domestic."

Piper smiled. "It's nice having someone to take care of, you know? I mean, someone besides my Anjovian ferns. Which reminds me, I need to stop by Aquaponics to check on the fronds. Graham, my old boss, sent me some from Greer, and I'm hoping I can propagate the species here. I do miss my work with the rare plants there."

As Piper talked about her work and starting at the aquaponics sector, they moved from the bar and walked down the promenade. She was listening to Piper and didn't realize how close they were to Abira until it was too late.

The small purple woman with yellow hair stopped both of them, holding out her hands. She frowned at each of them. "You must wear the charm for it to work."

Piper frowned. "I think I lost it in the struggle with Baxter Frink."

Hadley knew Piper well enough to know she was fibbing. She probably found the charm as unappealing as Hadley did.

"In that case, you must have another." Abira selected a charm for Piper and strung it with leather cord. "I'll bill the commander's account."

Piper looked less than grateful when she took the necklace and slipped it on. "Thanks. You're very thoughtful."

Hadley chuckled softly at that. Unfortunately, that turned Abira's lemon-yellow eyes on her, and she stiffened. She wanted to open her mouth and plead with Abira not to say anything, but it was too late.

"And where is your charm, Captain Wells? It must be worn at all times to prevent miscarriage and bring good luck to the baby. You most certainly want to wear it during delivery to ensure no pain."

Piper let out a soft gasp, and Hadley moaned. "I think I left it in my quarters."

"I should make you another then."

Hadley held up her hand to stop her. "No, that's okay. I'm heading to my quarters now anyway, and I'll get it then. Thank you for your thoughtfulness, Abira."

Abira look slightly miffed at losing out on another sale, but she nodded and wished them well as they headed on their way.

Hadley set a quick pace, hoping she could outrun the revelation and Piper's curiosity. Unfortunately, they soon reached the lift, and they were trapped in there together. There was no one else with them.

Piper hit the emergency stop button, and Hadley groaned. "I can't talk about it."

"Fine, but are you?" asked Piper with steel determination.

"Yes, I am. I didn't plan to be, but there it is. I don't know what I'm going to do. My career... I can't tell him..."

Piper was scowling. "That louse. He's left you in the situation, and he gets off without consequences. It's not fair. Someone should give him a talking-to."

Hadley groaned louder. "Please don't even think about it. He doesn't know, and that seems like the safest thing. I don't think he'll want to be involved, and even if he did, Krill could have me killed. You know he will if he finds out..." She glanced meaningfully at her stomach.

Piper sighed, looking somewhere between irritated and sad. "It's just not fair."

Hadley appreciated it, and she agreed one hundred percent with the sentiment. "It's not, but I did get myself into the situation."

Piper snorted. "I'd say you had some help in that department, though he's no help now. What a louse," she said again.

Oddly, she wanted to defend him, though there was no defense for his actions. He'd seduced her with clear intent, knowing all along he was going to marry another. He really was a louse, and any feelings she had for him needed to die quickly. "I'll put a picture of him on the dartboard in my room. That should be cathartic."

"And of his Lady Layala." Piper said with a bit of snark.

Hadley giggled at that, and the laugh turned into tears before she could help it. Piper hugged her, and though she had to bend down a bit to put her head against Piper's shoulder, she appreciated the comfort.

When the storm had passed, and the tears were no longer flowing, she lifted her head and stepped back. She swiped at her face. "How do I look?"

"Like you've been crying. Are you heading to your quarters for sure?"

Hadley nodded. "I don't really have duty today. I'm just going to try to relax and maybe not even think about anything, though I should be trying to think of a plan for the future."

"Take care of yourself, and call me any time you need me. And we're certainly going out for a girls' day of pampering soon." Piper released the hold on the lift, and it resumed moving. When they reached Hadley's floor, which was the same as Piper's, they stepped out. As they passed a waiting group, she heard them grumbling about the slowness of the lifts, and her lips twitched, but she was in no mood to be truly amused.

She was a little amused though when Piper walked her to her quarters before doubling back to the quarters she shared with Weston. She must really seem fragile right now.

Hadley let herself inside and sealed the door behind her. As soon as she did, she started stripping off her uniform as she made her way to the bathroom. A bracing shower helped restore calm and wash away the rest of the proof she'd been crying. When she looked at herself in the mirror a short time later, wrapped in a towel, she just looked like plain old Hadley. There was no sign yet of a swelling stomach, and no physical marks that reflected those marring her heart.

After her shower and slipping on a kimono, she entered the main part of her living quarters and saw her vid screen was flashing. She walked over to find she had three messages waiting. A quick review of the log revealed they were all from Nykal, and she deleted them unviewed.

She didn't need to know what line he was spinning now, and her best bet was to try to escape whatever hold he had on her. She couldn't do that if she let herself even view his messages. Just seeing his face was probably enough to seduce her again. She had to make sure that didn't happen anymore.

Chapter Six

IT HAD BEEN A LONG three days without a response to his messages. Nykal had sent more than he should, and each one had an increasingly desperate edge, practically begging her to respond. He could tell from the logs she hadn't even viewed them. That meant either she was deleting them as they came in, or there was something wrong with her.

If she were ill, she might not have gotten her messages. As much as he didn't want something to be wrong with her, he almost hoped that was the case rather than she was deliberately ignoring his missives. If she didn't want to hear from him or see his messages, that meant she was through with him. He couldn't stand the thought, and he suspected he was farther in the *viiraria* process than he'd estimated.

It was literally a compulsion he couldn't control as he paced through his quarters, searching for a solution. He tried to think of other ways to contact her, but the only one that would work for certain was to go in person. She couldn't delete *him* without looking at him.

There was so much pressure to stay though. There were a number of delicate negotiations to undertake, plus the usual duties. It all weighed heavily on him, and he cast a scathing glare at the crown that sat on the desk in the corner. He refused to wear the bloody thing unless he had to for public functions. All his resentment distilled down and focused on the crown. If he'd been standing right beside it, he probably would've picked it up and thrown it across the room.

He recognized the unsteadiness and clouding of his thoughts as withdrawal symptoms that he could attribute to the beginning stages of the *viiraria*. He needed to be with Hadley to calm himself and find equilibrium again. He needed to be with her on a permanent basis. He walked over to the database, tapping on his datapad as he looked for a way to keep her.

The planet's parliamentary agreement forbade any Jroj from propagating outside the species, but there was no explicit ban on relationships outside the species. He knew restrictions were tighter on him, as the Crown Prince, but he was searching for a way around it. He founded it in a historical archive rather than in a parliamentary document, and just knowing there was an option filled him with a semblance of peace—or at least left his thoughts clear enough to come up with a solid plan.

He raised Vasar on his wrist comm, and his brother's face appeared on the small screen. "Do you have a few moments to stop by my quarters? I'm in my private study."

Vasar nodded. "Of course."

With no further need to communicate that way, he ended the connection and waited for his brother. There was a knock at the door less than ten minutes later, and he walked over to open it. When his brother had slipped inside, he closed the door and locked it with his palm before leading his brother to the arrangement of seating in the corner. They sat down together, and he asked, "Would you like refreshments?"

Vasar shook his head. "No. I'm fine. What do you need, brother?"

"I have to go back to Olympus Station."

Vasar looked shocked. "Again already? I thought you handled the matter that drove you there last time. Isn't it something Ambassador Krill can deal with?"

As succinctly as possible, he explained his situation to his brother. He could see Vasar's sympathy, so he felt less awkward when he asked,

"Will you please step in for me for a few days to handle whatever needs to be done?"

"I'd be honored, as always. I wish you luck, Nykal." His expression seemed to suggest he thought his brother would need it.

Nykal thought so as well, since the solution he could offer Hadley probably wasn't one she'd love. He hoped being able to be together would be enough to convince her, especially if she felt as strongly for him as he did for her. He couldn't be sure of that after three days of silence though. "Thank you again."

Vasar nodded as he got to his feet. "I'm happy to help." He took a few steps and then turned back to face Nykal. "It occurs to me that you should have a Plan B."

Nykal nodded. "I should. What do you have in mind?"

With a calculating smile, Vasar returned to his seat and outlined his thoughts for Nykal. Nykal listened closely, nodding along in agreement as his brother laid out a simple, yet effective, plan. He was tempted to move it to his Plan A, it was so good.

NYKAL WAS DISPLEASED to see Krill waiting for him, since he hadn't given the ambassador any warning that he planned to be on the station for a few days. He'd deliberately omitted the information from Krill's channels, so someone had sent it along without his permission. That meant Krill was keeping tabs on him with the assistance of someone in his service.

He gritted his teeth as he approached the ambassador, whose frill was fully extended now, arcing up his skull in an impressive display. The other man drew himself to his full height, which was still a few inches shorter than Nykal, and he looked somewhat like a swollen orange *bindi*. The database provided an equivalent image as he had the thought, and he discovered a *bindi* was most similar to an Earth toad or a Volkarv *etig*.

"I didn't expect to see you here, Krill." His voice was less than friendly.

"And I didn't expect to see you. You should be back at the palace handling the duties of your position, Nykal." He didn't even bother with the title of Prince, which revealed how angry the other man was. "This is a clear breach of protocol, and you're breaking our laws by sleeping with a human."

Nykal started to brush past him as he said, "It's not your business."

Krill grabbed hold of his arm, arresting his progress. "If you don't return right now without seeing that worthless human again, I'll file charges against her for crimes against the crown. She'll then be extradited. Once she's convicted, she'll be executed. Her blood is on your hands."

Nykal stiffened, rage like he'd never known freezing him for an instant. When he finally got his jaw to unlock, he turned to fully face Krill. His hand gripped Krill's throat without his permission, and it took a moment for him to calm down enough not to squeeze his fingers closed around the thick column of muscle. "Mind your own business, or you'll find yourself up on charges of sedition and obstructing the crown. This isn't your business, and I won't have you meddling. I must be with her."

Krill's face betrayed no fear, but his eyes widened as if alarmed. "You haven't entered *viiraria* with her, have you?"

He didn't answer as he released his hold on the older man and stepped back. "Stay out of my way, Krill." Without another word to the ambassador, he walked away and went in search of Hadley.

Since she wasn't likely to welcome him if she was ignoring his messages, he waited near crew quarters as he'd done last time, trying to be more discreet this time. He didn't sit down and end up falling asleep.

He kept moving, and when the guards came through, they seemed to pay him no mind.

Neither of the guards were Hayes or Ipsy though, and he was relieved. While they would recognize him, both would probably insist on contacting Hadley, and if she was deliberately avoiding his messages as he suspected, he didn't want to give her a heads-up that he was here until he approached her.

At least two hours passed before he caught a glimpse of her sandy-brown hair, neatly confined in its usual twists. He waited until she was nearby before falling into step behind her. She remained oblivious to him for a second, and then she stiffened. She turned her head to scowl at him, and her anger was obvious. "What are you doing here?"

"I came to check on you. You aren't answering my messages. I need to see you."

She rolled her eyes. "You don't need anything from me, except a thrill in the bedroom. Just leave me alone."

He reached out to touch her arm, unable to resist the need to feel her physically. "Why are you angry with me?"

She sniffed at him. "You know."

He shook his head. "I don't. If you'll give me a short audience with you, maybe you can explain what's going on, and I can try to fix it."

She glared at him. "There's no fixing this." She started to pull away from him and keep walking, but he tightened his hold lightly. "Let go of me."

"In a second. I just wanted you to know that I'm not going anywhere. I'll stay here in the corridor if I have to, but you need to talk to me. I'll wait for however long it takes."

She let out a frustrated grunt and threw her hands in the air. "Fine. Five minutes." She looked around, apparently noticing the people moving back and forth. "I guess we should do this in my quarters."

It was clearly a grudging invitation, and she trudged forward like she carried a thousand pounds on her shoulders.

He was glad for any sort of invitation, grudging or otherwise. He had to get to the bottom of what was wrong.

She let him in her quarters seconds later, and he followed behind quickly before she could change her mind and close the panel in his face. Once they were inside, he relaxed marginally, though she seemed to grow stiffer. Her body language radiated rejection, and he was completely confused. "Why haven't you been answering my messages?"

"Because I haven't opened them."

He winced at her snappish tone. "Why haven't you opened them?"

"Can't you understand that we're through? This sex thing is over, and I'm done with you. Stop contacting me."

She sounded sincere, and she was clearly angry, but the wobble in her lips and the sadness in her eyes left him with a slight hope that maybe she didn't entirely mean it. "Why? What have I done?"

She rolled her eyes. "You know what you've done. I don't want to see you again."

He let out a sound of frustration. "I came here because I'm experiencing *viiraria* with you. It's the mating bond that develops in my people. I need to have you with me. I can't offer you the role of queen, but you could be my consort."

Her face turned purple. "Do you really think I'll give up my life here to come be your convenient whore? Get out now."

His eyes widened at her vitriol. "Please, don't misunderstand. Consort is just another title for wife, but one without official duties. It means you wouldn't be elevated to the role of queen, but you would still be considered my spouse. It's a position of honor, not one of sordidness."

She stilled, eyeing him warily. "So, it's not a mistress position?"

He shook his head. "Not at all. If you accept, we'll complete the *viiraria*, which eventually makes it possible not to be so consumed with each other, and you would be my honored companion. Your official title will be Lady, since you can't be queen without being Jroj."

"I have no interest in being queen." She shuddered as if the idea horrified her. "My life is here, and I'm not just going to give it up for the chance to be your *lady*." There was special bitterness in that word, and her anger seemed to stir to life again. "Besides, I doubt *Lady* Layala would appreciate you having a second wife."

He gulped. "You know about Layala?"

Her lips skinned back from her teeth, and she looked ferocious. "Yes, Krill made sure to tell me about her. You'll note the complete absence of you telling me about her? If you'd mentioned at any point during our interactions that you were engaged to another, there's no way you would've been in my bed, and I wouldn't be in this mess."

He tipped his head slightly. "What mess?"

She waved a hand. "Never mind. Just return to your betrothed. Forget all about me and don't come back."

He issued a heavy sigh. "I barely know Layala."

She was in the process of turning away from him, but she froze. When she looked over her shoulder, there was a hint of hope in her gaze. "If you barely know her, why are you marrying her?"

"It's common for lower-caste Jrojans to marry for love at their discretion, but royalty and nobility are still held hostage to the whims of Parliament. They make advantageous matches and declare who will marry whom. I've been betrothed to Layala since she was half a solar cycle, when I was barely four solar cycles myself. I've met her on four occasions. She seems pleasant enough, but I know nothing about her really. It's not required for me to know anything about her, at least according to Parliament. All that's required is I marry her as expected and perform my royal duties."

She stiffened. "Even if you don't love her, you're still going to marry her. I won't be your consort or piece on the side. Whatever you want to call it, it all boils down to the same thing. I refuse to be second-best."

He couldn't still the compulsion to reach out and stroke her cheek. She stiffened, but didn't move away. "You would never be second-best. You'll always be my first choice, and I promise if you agree to become my consort, I'll break the engagement with Layala."

She looked stunned. "How could I be your consort anyway? Krill says you're forbidden to date outside your species."

"We're forbidden to reproduce outside our species, but there's no official law on the books regarding having alien partners. I looked through the archives, and there's precedent for having a non-Jrojan as a consort. Three hundred solar cycles in our planet's past, one of the queens had a Baravyn consort. She also had a king, since she accepted her arranged marriage, but from what I pieced together, after she and her assigned spouse had a child, they both went their separate ways. Each took lovers, and her consort was her constant companion for most of the rest of her life, until he died before her. She died within weeks of his passing, and it was widely speculated to be from heartbreak."

She sighed. "But she still married the one Parliament picked for her. And what does your history tell you about the treatment her consort received?"

"It didn't touch on that, but it won't be easy. I can't promise that it would be. All I can promise is that I'll support you, and you'll be beside me."

"I don't think I can do that. Thank you for the offer, but it just won't work." She looked down, seeming to be examining her own bellybutton for a minute, or would be if her skin wasn't covered by her uniform. "Does Layala love you?"

He shrugged. "I don't see how, since we barely know each other."

"You're offering me an intangible impossibility. I should send you away right now, but I don't want to." Her expression changed, becoming more open and vulnerable as she moved closer. "I can give you tonight for sure, but no promises beyond that. We're too different, and there are too many obstacles in our way. We just can't—"

He could no longer stand to hear her pessimistic words. Each one was driving a stake through his heart, and his chest hurt from just the possibility of her refusing to come with him. He knew they should settle what was going on, and what they were going to do, but he couldn't think clearly with her so close.

Her arms wrapped around his neck, and he intensified the kiss. If all he had was tonight, he intended to use it to full advantage in an attempt to persuade her to accept becoming his consort. He lifted her into his arms and swept her off to bed, where they soon melted into one, and he could feel the binding of the *viiraria* tightening the link between them with each kiss and caress they shared.

Chapter Seven

NYKAL SHOWED NO SIGN of leaving that morning when she woke and got out of bed. She wished she didn't have to work, but the responsible thing to do was to continue as usual.

He stretched and blinked sleepy eyes at her when the bed shifted as she stood up. "You have to go so soon?"

She shrugged a shoulder. "I have to be on shift soon. Are you going to be here when I get off work?"

He gave her a lazy smile. "I'm sure Vasar will be happy to stand in for me for a few days. He's much more suited to the task than I am. I'll be here waiting for you and counting the seconds until you return."

She walked over to his side of the bed and leaned down to kiss him. It was meant to be a brief kiss, but soon turned passionate. Only when he tried to pull her onto the bed with him did she remember her obligations. She kept her spine straight and pulled back with a shake of her head. "I wish I could, but I can't."

He sighed, but nodded. "Believe it or not, I understand a thing or two about duty as well." He winked at her.

"I'll see if I can get away early, but probably not." She ran into the lavatory and saw to her morning ablutions as quickly as possible. She hoped to spend at least a few more minutes with him, so she rushed into her uniform before returning to the main living area.

He'd synthicated breakfast, and they enjoyed that together before she had to leave. She could certainly get used to this every morning, which was a dangerous thought. There couldn't be an *every morning* with him. He might be able to have her as a consort, but their child was forbidden by Jroj law, and that was an obstacle she couldn't remove and refused to consider doing so.

"I have to go now." She blew him a kiss to keep distance from him, so she could bear to walk out of her quarters. Then she joined the flow of foot traffic headed toward the lift to get to the command deck. Her thoughts were occupied with Nykal's surprise arrival, and the knowledge that he was technically betrothed, but had no interest in marrying Layala. If he'd only met his future wife a few times, she could understand why. His offer of consort wasn't exactly what she wanted either, but it was certainly better than mistress.

How was she going to tell him about the baby? Should she? She still had no idea. More than once last night, when they'd been so close and enmeshed in each other's arms, she'd been on the brink of telling him she was pregnant. Each time, fear had held her back.

She was afraid of his reaction, and afraid of having to give up her life at the station, but mostly she was afraid of Krill and the repercussions he could bring down upon her. She wanted to think Nykal wielded more power, but after seeing Krill's machinations, she doubted a man who'd only been Crown Prince for ten solar cycles was up to the political maneuvers of someone like Krill. He would do everything in his power to keep her away from Nykal, and he'd most likely want to ensure her child was never born. She couldn't allow that.

At first, it was a simple day, at least as far as being second-in-command of a station the size of Olympus could ever be simple. There were no deviations from tasks that she'd done a thousand times before, at least until midmorning. Her wrist comm beeped when she was negotiating a labor dispute in the water-purification sector.

When she pressed the button, Weston's face filled the small screen. "Yes, Commander?" They were friendly enough to be on a first-name basis when they weren't at work, but they always kept things strictly professional when representing Olympus Station.

"There's an unexpected dignitary visiting, and I'd like you to help greet her. Can you meet me at the docking bay in twenty minutes?"

She quickly evaluated how soon she could wrap up the task here. "That should be doable. I'll see you soon." She disconnected and resumed negotiations with the supervisor and three of the workers, who felt mistreated. She listened to their complaints, finding herself siding with the workers, but she couldn't help being curious about who the visiting dignitary might be.

Occasionally they had unexpected visits, usually from famous people who wanted no record of their travels recorded anywhere until after they'd already left. Once, they'd gotten a famous musician from the Kurgitti system, and she'd favored the staff with a private concert. She'd also hit some very sharp notes, and Hadley winced just thinking about it.

"Well, what do you think, Captain Wells? Are you going to order them back to work?" The supervisor looked smug.

She nodded slowly, absorbing the disappointed expressions of the workers. "I am, but with caveats. For one thing, you know you're extending the hours that they're contracted to work. They have a valid complaint about that, and if you must do it, you'll compensate them double."

He scowled. "That comes out of my budget."

She quickly pulled up his budget, seeing he always had an excess at the end of each solar cycle. It appeared to be a point of pride for him. "You have plenty of funds in your budget. I understand you're a conservatively fiscal man, but we have to pay our workers well. Is everyone agreed?" The workers nodded, and the supervisor eventually gave a sharp incline of his head that revealed his reluctance, but he didn't protest.

After that, she started jogging toward the docking bay, since it had taken a little longer to wrap up than she'd expected. She had to stop quickly though, because it made nausea churn in her stomach. She paused to lean against the wall as a wave of dizziness swept over her.

"Are you all right, Captain?" asked a feminine voice.

She looked over her shoulder and saw the guard she recognized as Ipsy, who had contacted her about Nykal waiting for her in the crew quarters section. An older man stood behind her, and he looked vaguely concerned as well.

She nodded. "I think I just ran too quickly and skipped breakfast." The lie slipped almost smoothly off her tongue, though she wasn't accustomed to telling falsehoods. She took a deep breath and continued on, finding she was fine as long as she only walked quickly and didn't run.

That put her late, and she reached the greeting area a couple of minutes past when Weston had requested her arrival. At first, she saw only Weston's back, but as she got closer, she recognized Ambassador Krill standing on his left. She smothered a groan as she took a step up to stand beside Weston. She was quiet for a moment until conversation stopped, and then she looked at the commander. "I apologize for being late, sir. The task I was handling took a little longer than expected."

"That's fine, Captain Wells. Allow me to introduce Lady Layala Drestin. She's the prince's betrothed."

Her lips felt numb as she turned to face Layala, who was a stunning woman with exotic features. With her orange skin and faint black striping, adorned with a long curtain of glossy black hair, Hadley wondered how Nykal could resist temptation. Uncertain of the protocol, she treated Layala like she was a princess as she bent at the waist. "Welcome to Olympus Station, Lady Drestin."

"The correct title is Lady Layala—until she becomes Queen Atole." Krill's eyes gleamed cruelly with the correction.

"Thank you. I've heard all about the station. And you." Layala glowered at her for a moment before turning a pleasant expression to

Weston. "Perhaps Captain Wells would like to give me a tour of the facilities?" asked Layala in a perfectly dulcet tone.

"I'd be happy to," said Hadley through gritted teeth.

Before Weston could confirm or deny that request, Nykal suddenly appeared. "Layala, I didn't expect you." He shot a glare at Krill. "It's a good thing my crew alerted me to your presence."

Layala nodded her head, and her reaction to him was difficult to interpret. She seemed to find him as interesting as a lump of clay, yet she screamed jealousy when she looked at Hadley. It was confusing.

"I had an unexpected opportunity to visit, Nykal."

That she addressed the prince by his first name must mean they were on fairly equal footing, which made sense if they were engaged. Hadley knew they were, and it cut through her heart, though there wasn't must much chemistry between them.

"Since the prince is here, perhaps he could see to that duty? I really need Captain Wells's assistance." Weston nodded at Layala and Krill again before turning to nod to Nykal. "We must have a reception to greet you tomorrow evening, Lady Layala, if that's convenient for you, of course?"

"I'm sure it's most convenient. My schedule remains fairly open while I deal with an unpleasant task."

Weston didn't say anything to that other than, "Good luck with your business." Then he turned to Hadley. "Please join me on the command deck, Captain Wells."

Her stomach churned with nausea again, and she wasn't certain whether it was from emotional turmoil, nervousness, or normal morning sickness. She followed Weston to the lift, and when they stepped on, she groaned under her breath to see they were only ones using it.

They'd gone up half a floor before he reached over and pressed the emergency stop button. She almost commented that he was just like Piper, but she held in that remark. She didn't want to get Piper in trouble if Weston had figured out she was entangled in a potential incident, and Piper had known.

"Tell me what's going on here, Captain Wells."

She shuddered at his firm tone and his use of her formal title even when it was just the two of them. Pushing back her shoulders, she straightened her spine and said, "It's a personal matter, Commander. I can handle it."

His eyebrows drew together as he frowned. "Can you really? Do you require my assistance?"

She started to decline, and then she shrugged. "I'm not sure, to be honest. It's a delicate matter, and I'm embarrassed to discuss it, but Ambassador Krill might try to cause problems for me and for Nykal." That revealed enough about what was going on, didn't it?

It seemed to give Weston enough information, because he nodded and released the emergency stop button. "I'll be nearby at the reception, and if you need anything, feel free to find me. I'll help you if I can. You're a good friend, Hadley."

"So are you, Weston, and I appreciate the concern. Thank you."

He shot her a glance from the corner of his eye as the lift reached the command deck's floor. "I suppose your secret might be the reason Piper's been carefully screening her words?"

Her eyes widened as they stepped out. "How did you know?"

"I know her well enough to tell when she's trying not to tell me something. That, combined with Ambassador Krill specifically requesting your presence to greet Lady Layala, helped me put together some of the issue. I'm sure Piper will be relieved to know she doesn't have to guard every word now."

Hadley felt guilty. "I'm sorry to put her in that position, sir. I shouldn't have taken her into my confidence, or I should've given her permission to share. I actually expected her to, because you're so close."

He smiled. "We are close, and I love her beyond reason, but she's also your loyal friend, and she wouldn't betray that lightly."

That made Hadley feel good, and she nodded at him. "Did you really require my assistance for anything, Commander?"

He flashed her a mischievous grin. "As a matter of fact, I have a stack of Z24-R reports that need to be processed and filed before the end of the day. I'd like to leave early, so I could use your assistance with that."

She groaned, feeling like she'd been had. "Aw, those things are tedious, and why does the Coalition insist on maintaining paper copies too? I feel like I'm being punished, Commander."

He chuckled as he led the way to his office, lifting half the pile of reports to hand to her. "So do I every time I have to fill these out."

HADLEY DIDN'T MANAGE to get off early, but she was on time when she reached her quarters. Nykal was waiting for her, and he'd synthicated dinner. She didn't bother to change first, since her stomach was rumbling. The nausea had finally faded a couple of hours ago, and now she felt like she could eat again. He'd picked one of her favorite meals, likely checking her order history, and he had something she'd never seen before. "What's that?"

"It's Jroj *mermit* bass with sautéed *vlomit* bulbs. Would you like a taste?"

She nodded, taking the bite he offered. It was unusual, but certainly not terrible. "Is that your native cuisine?"

He smiled. "Not so much these days. I suspect the Coalition is just processing information in chronological order to put into the databanks. This is something our ancestors would've eaten more commonly than we do, especially since the *vlomit* flowers have been extinct for two hundred solar cycles, but it's very good."

She eyed the bulbs. "I wonder if that's how they really tasted? The Coalition would've analyzed the phytochemical profile to reach its best estimate of the taste."

He shrugged. "It's as close as I'll get to *vlomit* bulbs." His expression changed. "Are you all right? I know today was stressful."

"I'm fine."

"Was the commander harsh with you?" He seemed protective.

She shook her head. "No, not at all. He just offered his help if we need it." She reached for the glass of water, once more disdaining the Denariian wine that he seemed to so enjoy. She liked it well enough herself, but obviously couldn't drink it now. "May I ask you something?" At his nod, she asked, "What happens if you don't marry Lady Layala, or if you choose me as your consort?"

His expression betrayed nothing when he said, "Parliament will probably depose me, and then they'll appoint a new king."

She frowned. "I can't let you give up your throne. You have to marry Layala, don't you?"

He scowled. "I won't. I had no plans to marry her before I met you, since I refuse to marry someone I barely know and don't love. Besides, my brother, Vasar, has an affection for Lady Layala of which she remains unaware. I couldn't do that to my brother, since we're close."

She frowned at the news. "But what will you do then?"

He shrugged. "I've asked my brother to join me here at Olympus Station, and he and I will decide a plan together. And you're welcome to strategize with us."

She hesitated and then shook her head. "I don't understand enough about your home world and your politics to be much help."

He reached across the table and took her hand. "Just having you at my side is ample help, Hadley. I never expected to meet anyone like you, and I'm grateful that I have."

She nodded, blinking back tears. She was on the verge of telling him about the baby, but she held back. Until they had a firm plan or way to proceed, she wasn't confident that Krill wouldn't find a way to undo whatever they came up with. Until it was safe, she couldn't tell him about the child, though the knowledge was eating her alive with guilt at keeping it to herself.

Chapter Eight

THEY ARRIVED AT THE reception on time the next evening, and Nykal insisted on entering with her. His brother Vasar brought up the rear, and he proved to be a younger, less interesting version of his brother, at least to her.

Hadley had broken protocol slightly by opting for an evening dress instead of her usual dress uniform. She was already breaking so many rules that it seemed like a minor one, and she wanted to take advantage of the opportunity to dress up to impress Nykal—and also to keep Lady Layala from completely outshining her.

She wasn't at all surprised to see the woman had dressed with obvious care. Tonight, she wore a gown that looked like spun silver, but was somehow opaque enough to hide her form. That was disappointing, since she'd been anxious to see how an alien with four breasts looked in a dress, but the top was too boxy to reveal much.

She couldn't deny Lady Layala was an unusual and exotic mix, and Hadley would never be that. She was on the quieter side, with what she considered above-average looks, but they seemed to please Nykal. She reminded herself it wasn't a contest between herself and Layala. She had no need to win Nykal's attention from her, since he had no affection for the Lady. He had respect, but nothing else.

Since she'd worked most of the day, she had missed Vasar and Nykal's strategizing session, but she knew part of their plan was to make it plain to Lady Layala that Vasar had an affection for her. She wasn't entirely certain how that would help, but the brothers seemed to believe it would be a sound strategy, so she supported it.

They reached the table where the commander waited with Lady Layala and the ambassador. This was a smaller, more intimate gathering than the last one she attended before the night she spent with Nykal. They also didn't have to worry about someone trying to kill Piper now.

She nodded a greeting to everyone and mentioned formal titles before sitting down beside Piper. Nykal took the chair beside her, and Vasar took the one beside him, which put him directly beside Layala. She seemed put-out at that, and Krill looked completely annoyed. His frill was starting to creep up.

Piper was looking at Krill. "Would it be impolite to ask you a perhaps culturally sensitive question, Ambassador Krill?"

He frowned, as though deep in thought, before shaking his head. "Go ahead, please, Mrs. Templeton."

Piper apparently didn't feel the need to let him know the wedding hadn't happened yet. "It's perhaps a little delicate, so if I'm overstepping, please feel free to tell me. I just wondered why you have a frill, and yet Prince Nykal doesn't appear to. And neither does Prince Vasar?" She asked that with a cocked eyebrow in Vasar's direction.

Vasar shook his head as Krill cleared his throat. "Just like among humans, there are various races in our species. Some of us are born with frills, and some are born with hair." Krill seemed unbothered by the question.

Hadley was surprised at his diplomatic response, but Piper had been gentle when asking, and she wasn't interested in the prince, so offered no threat to the line of succession.

Talk was casual as dinner progressed, and Hadley did her best to tap dance around Layala's pointed questions, while Nykal was going out of his way to highlight Vasar's achievements and talk up his brother. Layala didn't seem to notice. She was too fixated on Hadley, and

Hadley knew she had to get the confrontation out of the way. She stood up. "If you'll excuse me, I need to visit the facilities."

It wasn't at all surprising when Layala stood up as well. "Would you be so kind as to show me where they are, Captain Wells?"

She was aware of Nykal casually squeezing her hand for strength as she nodded at the woman and gestured her forward. They walked in silence until they were away from the table, and Hadley prepared herself for Layala's searing words. To her surprise, the other woman didn't say anything until they reached the facilities.

"Ambassador Krill told me all about you."

Hadley nodded. "I'm certain he's given the foulest interpretation he can."

Layala frowned. "He told me you're plotting to get Nykal to give up his throne, since you know you can never be the queen."

Hadley blinked. "That's not true, but I'm not surprised he told you that. May I ask you a question?"

Layala stiffened, but nodded.

"Do you care about Nykal, or just his throne?"

Dark orange spots appeared on her cheeks. "I've been training to be his queen since I was an infant. My life is entwined with his."

Hadley leaned against the sink. "But do you love him?"

Layala frowned. "I barely know him, though I know all of his preferences. How can I love him? And why would it matter either way?"

Hadley decided it was time to be bluntly honest. "Because I love Nykal, and I suspect he loves me, though we haven't said the words yet. I'm not trying to get him to give up his crown, or to hurt you. I can't help loving him, and he can't help loving me. So, if you're here because you love Nykal, that puts a different complexion on things than if you're just here to preserve your crown."

Layala didn't seem to grasp the difference. "I'm here to ensure I'll be the queen."

"Did you know Vasar has an affection for you?" She used the term Nykal had used last night, assuming it was a common one in their culture.

Layala's mouth dropped open, and she looked stunned. "Vasar? He has an affection for me?" Her cheeks flushed again, but she didn't seem angry this time. "I know Vasar very well. We attended many of the same etiquette classes, since we're the same age, and they were preparing me for integration into the Atole family."

"Apparently, you made quite an impression on the younger prince. I don't know how strong his affection is, but I know it's a lot stronger than what you'd find with Nykal." She softened her tone. "I'm not trying to get you to accept second-best. I'm just pointing out that if you could find love with your spouse, wouldn't it be better than tepid friendship like you'd have with Nykal?" That would be worth any crown to Hadley, but she hadn't endured the same upbringing as Layala.

Layala didn't really commit to that. She just stared at Hadley for a moment before nodding. "We should return to the reception before they start to wonder where we are."

Hadley nodded. "I'll be there shortly. I really do need to use the facilities." That was one of the *joys* of pregnancy that she had started to notice the last few days. It probably had something to do with her child gestating faster than a human baby would, so she was getting more of the side effects earlier.

As soon as Layala left the room, she hurried to the nearest stall. When she was done, she washed her hands, splashed her face, and returned to the reception. Dinner was waiting for them, and as Hadley sat down, she caught the scent of something that smelled like hummus. It didn't really look like hummus, but it had the same sort of aroma, and her stomach protested. She started to feel dizzy, and she leaned back in her seat to fan herself.

"Hadley, what's wrong?" Nykal leaned forward, clearly anxious. "You've gone so pale."

She tried to summon a smile. "I'm fine. Perhaps just a little overheated." She barely bit down a gag when the scent of the food assaulted her all over again as she shifted in her chair.

"You must call for your medical person," said Nykal with a note of authority as he spoke to Weston.

Hadley wanted to tell him not to bother, but she was too busy trying to choke down vomit. The last thing she wanted to do was vomit at the reception in Lady Layala's honor.

Gretel soon appeared, and she did a quick scan before handing Hadley a little disk. "Melt this under your tongue, and it will help with nausea. Come by Medical tomorrow, and I'll make sure you have a supply for the next few weeks."

Despite Gretel's attempt to be discreet, they seemed to have gathered a crowd around them, and Nykal looked frantic when he asked, "Is she ill?"

"Not overly so," said Gretel, looking torn. She was probably trying to give an answer that hid the truth. Hadley appreciated her effort.

"You said she was going to be ill for weeks. What's going on?"

Neither Gretel nor Hadley answered, but it was Layala who put it all together. She let out a gasp and asked, "Are you pregnant?"

Hadley still didn't answer, though her lack of answer seemed sufficient for everyone. A small babble of voices filled the table, but it was Krill's that cut through when he leapt to his feet and shouted at Nykal. His frill was fully erect now, and he was a bright orange. "You must assure me that problem isn't yours, Prince Nykal."

With a defiant air, Nykal put his hand over Hadley's stomach. "I don't consider it a problem." He looked at her, and there was a hint of betrayal in his expression, but it didn't come through his voice. "I'm just learning about it, but I have no intention of disavowing my child."

Krill let out a shrieking sound before his attention turned to Hadley. "Then you must insist he's not the father. Tell him he's not, Wells."

She opened her mouth, fear nudging her toward that direction, but she couldn't do it. She couldn't blatantly lie to him about their baby. She looked away from Krill and didn't answer him. Instead, she reached out to put a hand on Nykal's cheek. "I'm so sorry I didn't tell you sooner. I didn't know how, and I was afraid. Certain threats were made..." She darted her gaze back to Krill before looking at Nykal again. "I was trying to protect the baby."

"You must disavow this now." Krill made the request in a commanding fashion as he glared at Nykal.

"I won't. You've heard the last word on the matter, Krill. This isn't your business and isn't up for discussion."

With that same shriek of frustration, Krill stormed from the reception room. Hadley was still feeling shaky, though the nausea medicine was already working after she'd melted it under her tongue. Food even seemed appealing then, and her stomach grumbled with hunger. She giggled softly, feeling embarrassed. "I apologize."

"There's no reason to be sorry. That's perfectly natural." Gretel winked at her.

"Would you care to join us, Gretel?" asked Weston with the faintest trace of a grin. "We seem to have prematurely lost a dinner guest."

Hadley could only imagine the horrible impression Layala was getting of the station crew. She shot a cautious glance at Layala, and she was surprised to find that rather than glaring at her and Nykal, she was immersed in quiet conversation with Vasar. There was a true smile on Layala's lips, and she seemed happy for the first time since she'd arrived at Olympus Station. That was difficult to judge without knowing her, but it was certainly the first time she'd seen Layala smile since she met her yesterday

As dinner progressed, she leaned over and quietly asked Nykal, "Are we in big trouble?"

"Krill will probably try to stir up contention, but I'm not worried." He truly looked sanguine about the whole thing.

She wanted to trust in him, since he had greater knowledge of Krill and his culture, but she couldn't help a prickling sense of fear that lingered in the back of her mind. Long after the reception had ended, and she was lying in Nykal's arms later, with his hand against her belly as he slept, she was still worrying about the consequences and fearing what Krill might do.

Chapter Nine

HE WOKE EARLY THAT morning, and she was still sleeping peacefully in his arms. Nykal's hand had remained across her belly while they slept, and he marveled once more they had created life together against all the odds. It would be complicated, but he had to trust that his and Vasar's plan would work. It must. There was no way he would disavow her or his child, especially not for the sake of a crown he didn't want anyway.

She startled sleepily, and her hair spread out over his chest. He lifted a handful and threaded it through his fingers, admiring the silky smoothness. Her eyelashes started to flutter, and when she looked up at him, she frowned instead of smiling. That made him frown. "What displeases you?"

She blinked and then a tentative smile formed on her lips. "I'm sorry. I think I just got another bout of guilt. I wanted so badly to tell you, but—"

He put his finger against her lips. "We settled this last night, first at the dinner, and then later before our lovemaking. I understand why you didn't tell me sooner, and I'm happy to know. We don't have to discuss it again, unless you absolutely must."

After a brief hesitation, she shook her head. "No, I'd really like to get past the guilty feeling. So, tell me more about this *viiraria* thing."

He shrugged. "It's a pheromonal bonding of our people. I'm surprised it actually works with someone who isn't Jroj, since the biology is different, but it seems to have the same effect, at least on me.

I know it doesn't on you, but it brings me closer to you each moment we spend together."

She nibbled on her lower lip, looking worried. "Is it just a pheromone thing? I mean, is it a biological compulsion you can't ignore?"

He frowned for a moment, understanding there was more to her question than the basic words, but not sure what she wanted. Suddenly, it occurred to him. "You're concerned that I'm biologically driven to mate with you, but not emotionally?" At her nod, he ran his hand through her hair again, while his other one splayed wider across her tummy.

"You don't have to fear that. *Viiraria* can only start to develop when there's already an emotional attachment and an attraction between partners. Otherwise, it would be inconvenient to develop an affection for someone that turned into *viiraria* without them being an active participant. It's very much on both partners' side in my culture, but it only grows if there's love starting."

She let out a long breath, clearly relieved. "I told Layala last night that I'm falling in love with you, and I suspected it's the same for you." Her lids drooped, veiling her eyes with her lashes. Her cheeks flushed slightly, and when she opened her eyes wide again, she looked apprehensive. "I lied though."

He scowled. "You don't feel an affection for me?"

Her eyes widened. "Oh, no. I didn't mean it that way. I told her I was falling, but the truth is, I've already fallen completely in love with you. I swear it happened the moment I saw you across the docking bay, but I tried to deny it. It sounds so silly to say I fell in love with you the moment I saw you."

"Then I must be silly as well, because I felt the same sensation. It was like something pulling me toward you, and nothing could get in the way."

His words must have pleased her, because she curled closer and practically purred her pleasure. "Do I have to do anything special for your *viiraria* bonding thing?"

He chuckled at her constant reference to it as a *thing*. "No, other than staying as close to me as you can. I'll need that constant contact with you for at least several months."

She made a satisfied sound as she moved closer. "That shouldn't be a problem, aside from when I'm at work. I can't seem to get enough of you, and being away from you is unpleasant. I'm afraid I can't take a leave-of-absence from work or come with you to Jroj, so how are we going to make this work?"

He opened his mouth to tell her when the alarm she'd set last night started ringing. He sighed. "We need to see Layala and Vasar off for their departure."

It was obvious she was disappointed at the interruption, and she clearly had questions. He wished he could explain his strategy to her, but until he knew if it would work, he was afraid to raise her hopes. If this plan didn't work, he would find another way to have her, but he hadn't figured out his next plan just yet, should it be needed.

"Are you going back with them this morning?" Her white-knuckled grip on the bedsheet revealed her anxiety.

"Not yet." That was the best he could do until he saw their plan to fruition.

They were soon dressed and hurried toward the docking bay, arriving a short time later. As they stepped onto the platform, he caught sight of Layala boarding the ship. His brother stood at the bottom of the ramp, and he looked upset. It was natural for him to rush forward to see what had bothered his brother. He put a hand on his shoulder as his younger brother faced off with an older man wearing the designation of Colonel in their militia. "Vasar, what has you troubled?"

"Colonel Goivaise seems to believe he's going to arrest you and Hadley to return to Jroj to face charges." Vasar was practically vibrating with rage.

Nykal embraced that same emotion as he imagined them clamping restraints on his mate and dragging her up the boarding ramp to return to the planet to execute her with his child inside her. He skinned his lips back to show his teeth. "You won't touch her."

Colonel Goivaise looked troubled, but he held out a datapad. "I have an extradition request for the human Hadley Wells, and I also have a warrant for your arrest, Your Highness. I'm supposed to take you discreetly, but I'm authorized to do what's required, if I must."

Hadley stepped forward to join him then, and Nykal put out an arm to shield her. "Hadley, you must leave right now."

She stayed stubbornly in place. "I've already called Weston, and he's on his way."

"Your commander will have no jurisdiction over Jrojan matters," said Krill as he stepped forward, clearly in his element. If he swelled any more with spite, he might explode. "I warned you of the consequences. Now you'll pay them. Unless the prince comes to his senses, he'll pay them as well."

Nykal turned from the colonel, launching himself toward Krill. If it hadn't been for Hadley getting in his way, deliberately blocking him, his hands would already be around the other man's neck. A savage thrill of glee shot through him at the idea of strangling Krill, though it felt foreign. Their race was peaceful and had been for hundreds of solar cycles, but he understood the bloodlust then that had once dominated their ancestors.

"It's okay, Nykal. He isn't worth it." Hadley's hands on his face and her soothing tone as she looked up at him got through to him.

He conquered his anger and stepped back, putting his arm around her to pull her with him. He ignored Krill and faced the colonel "I won't go with you, and I certainly won't let you take Hadley."

Goivaise looked uneasy. "It's not my intention to make this an incident, Your Highness. I have orders I must follow."

"Those orders are directly contradictory to what I'll do or allow."

Before the colonel could retort, there was a rush of feet, and Nykal looked over his shoulder at the arrival of Commander Templeton. His eyes widened slightly when he saw a contingent of at least twenty of the station guards standing behind Weston.

He gulped softly, knowing if Weston chose their side, the guards were a good thing. If he chose to accept the extradition order, they could be used to leverage both him and Hadley onto the ship. He couldn't imagine the commander doing that to his second-in-command, but he was wary.

Krill stepped forward, oozing his way toward the commander with supercilious malice, but making a wide arc around Nykal, who could've reached out and grabbed him with a slight lunge. When he stood beside Weston, his frill started to rise. "This has nothing to do with you, Commander, and it isn't the station's business. The prince and the human have both violated Parliamentary law, and now they face the consequences."

Weston's expression revealed little about his leanings, but his tone was firm. "Interesting. Neither Nykal nor Hadley have broken any Coalition laws while on the station."

"Colonel Goivaise, show him the extradition order," said Krill imperiously, as though he were the prince instead of Nykal.

As the colonel started to step forward, Weston raised a hand. "You can transmit it electronically for the records. I have no need to look at it today, because Captain Wells is a resident of Olympus Station, and I'm prepared to offer Prince Nykal refugee status and asylum here on Olympus Station as well."

Krill swelled up and looked like he was about to hop up and down in anger, just like a *bindi*. "You can't do that, Commander. You risk the treaty between our world and the Coalition."

"I'm sure this could provoke tensions, but I believe you should review the agreement your Parliament signed when you joined the Coalition. You're bound to a trade agreement for five solar cycles, and any disputes must be settled through mediation overseen by an independent party not representing Jroj or the Coalition.

"What? That's outrageous."

Ignoring Krill's interruption, Weston continued, "You're welcome to request mediation, but you're not arresting Hadley or Nykal today, and not ever if I can do anything to prevent it. They've done nothing the Coalition considers a crime. While your sovereign rules apply when Coalition people are on your planet, you should have read enough of the agreement to know that you agree to follow Coalition guidelines when you're visiting Coalition-held territory. Prince Nykal didn't violate those rules, and Captain Wells has never stepped foot on your planet."

"You won't get away with this. I'll have you brought up on charges too, Templeton." Krill's frill trembled in his rage.

Once more, Weston didn't respond to Krill's words, other than to ask, "Would you like to return to Jroj on this ship, Ambassador Krill? I assume you're going to be uncomfortable here on Olympus Station while awaiting mediation. I believe the process of opening a case and getting a mediator can take several rotations. Perhaps even a full solar cycle."

Nykal grinned at the diplomatic way Weston phrased his request for Krill to leave.

Krill deflated for a moment, looking shocked. Then he squared his shoulders again, and his frill stopped shaking. "You'll regret this, Templeton." He swept past Nykal and Hadley, pausing to grimace at her. His disdainful glance settled on her stomach, and he shuddered. "That thing won't be born. Mark my words."

That was more than Nykal could stand, and he lunged forward after ensuring she was steady on her feet, taking a mad swing at Krill.

The colonel and his brother blocked him, keeping him from acting so rashly, and they held him back until he'd calmed.

After a moment of heavy breathing, he finally managed to regain control. "I apologize. I'm not used to behaving like a barbarian, but that man…" He trailed off with a scowl at Krill, who had scurried up the boarding ramp and now stood at the entryway to the ship.

"Don't let him make you act like an animal, Your Highness," said Goivaise. There was sympathy in his gaze when he nodded at Nykal.

"Do you want me to stay?" asked Vasar, looking concerned.

Nykal shook his head. "Stick with the plan, brother."

After a hug, Vasar hurried up the boarding ramp, shoving past Krill without even looking at him.

"Good luck, Your Highness," said Goivaise.

As he turned and walked up the boarding ramp, Krill swelled again. "What are you doing? Arrest them."

The colonel shook his head. "I have a Parliamentary order, but Commander Templeton has final say in Coalition territory. You'll have to do as he suggested and set in motion the process of mediation."

Krill was still stuttering in his rage as Goivaise not-so-gently maneuvered him onto the ship, and the boarding ramp started to close behind them, slowly lifting. They could hear Krill screeching in protest as it slammed shut, finally blocking out the noise.

He turned to Hadley, frowning. "I'm sorry about this mess, and I'm sorry I lost my temper in front of you. I promise that isn't like me at all, and I'd never hurt you."

"I know that."

He realized she was trembling all over. "It's all right." Her teeth were chattering, and he doubted she was cold. She seemed to be going into shock, and he supposed the emotional trauma might trigger such a response. He swooped forward and lifted her into his arms. He turned to Weston, who still stood with his guards behind him. "What's the fastest way to Medical?"

Weston broke into a run ahead of him, leading the way. It seemed to take forever to reach that section, though it wasn't more than two or three minutes. He left her after a few minutes, when Gretel suggested she needed a light sedative and some rest. He would've liked to stay with her and watch over her while she slept, but he knew she was safe now, and he had things to which he must attend.

He went to the public communications area on the promenade deck, since he didn't yet have access to Hadley's quarters without her permission. If he was going to stay on Olympus Station, and it seemed like he was, he would have to ask her to grant him access privileges.

In the meantime, he chose a soundproof booth and linked to one of the communication arrays. Olympus Station included three powerful ansibles that could boost the signal to just about anywhere in their galaxy, so he had no trouble reaching Parliament.

He was unsurprised to find Krill conferenced in as well, though he was still on the ship *en route* to the home world. He glared at the thirty-six members of Parliament, who dictated the decisions of so many lives on Jroj. He didn't speak to them as he glowered, making sure his gaze touched on each one of them.

Primary Minister Srgren stepped forward slightly, looking servile, and yet simultaneously self-righteous. It was a unique combination, but the politician seemed to have mastered it. "Your Highness, you should be on the way to the planet to face charges right now. Ambassador Krill's disturbing news constitutes a Parliamentary crisis, and he tells us you refused to board the ship to return to Palos. That must be a mistake?"

"Krill tells the truth for a change. Commander Templeton has offered me asylum here."

"You would involve outsiders in a Parliamentary matter?" Srgren looked as swollen as Krill. "Unacceptable. Return at once."

"No." He didn't offer a long protest or explanation.

"Trying to hide from this won't work. The Coalition will never allow it. You'll be extradited here. You should return now and make it easier on yourself. If you don't, you'll be a fugitive and make it even worse on yourself...and the human," he added with a sly inflection.

He glared. "I won't return as long as you're trying to dictate my life. I've broken an archaic law written when our people first realized we weren't alone in the galaxies. It needs to be repealed. I won't apologize or face charges for following my heart. All I've done is fall in love."

"With a non-Jroj," said the primary minister as his face turned an angry dark-orange.

"And she's pregnant," said Krill with an air of angry delight, making it clear he hadn't yet revealed that information.

There were gasps of shock among Parliament, and Nykal braced himself for their ugliness. He was temporally distracted by a beeping sound indicating someone was requesting entry. He started to ignore it until the A.I. brought up the image of Hadley standing outside the cubicle.

With a frown of surprise, he released the lock with his palm, and she entered before closing it behind herself and locking it again. He ignored Parliament for a moment to stare up at her, noticing her color was better. "I thought you were resting?"

She put a hand on his shoulder. "Gretel started to give me a mild sedative, but it turned out I didn't really need it. I was able to regain control, and I knew you had this problem to face." Her gaze touched lightly on the screen, though she didn't seem to be looking at any of Parliament. "I couldn't let you do it alone."

He put his hand over hers on his shoulder and returned his attention to Parliament. "There won't be any negotiation, and there'll be no charges filed. This ends today."

"That isn't how it works, Your Highness. You don't dictate to Parliament," said Srgren with a sickening air of superiority. "You hold the position of leadership, but it's all a front. True power lies with Parliament, and you know it."

"I know I'm sick of you trying to dictate to me. I'm going to marry Hadley, and I'm going to raise our child with her. I don't care what you think. Neither of us have broken Coalition or Olympus laws."

"If you persist in this defiance, you'll be stripped of your crown and banished from our home world." The primary minister seemed to think that was all the threat he needed.

"I realize that."

Hadley gasped. "You didn't tell me they would banish you. You can't do this." She said the words softly enough that Parliament didn't seem to overhear.

He just brushed a finger against his lip, indicating she shouldn't say anything for a moment. Timing was critical, and they were approaching the moment. The message to Vasar was already composed and would be transmitted in seconds.

Parliament muted the screen for a moment, and though he could see them frantically talking, and some gesticulating wildly, he couldn't hear the conversation. That suited him fine, because he could imagine they were reviewing their options and trying to find the soundest strategy for moving forward. If he had any regard for any of them, he would've almost felt sorry for them to be in this position. They still thought they had a possibility of winning, and they were bound to be humiliated in a crushing defeat soon. He tried not to smile at that.

The silence ended soon, and he could hear them talking again, though in whispers now as the primary minister stepped forward again to face the screen. "We've come to an agreement, Your Highness. If you disavow any connection to the human and return right now, prepared to marry Lady Layala this very day, all charges against your paramour will be dismissed, and we'll quietly cancel your arrest warrant. We don't need the upheaval of our Crown Prince splitting apart the country."

"That's an interesting proposal, but I have a better one," said Nykal.

As perfectly timed as they had practiced, his brother Vasar suddenly joined the conversation, his image appearing on the screen as he was routed through Olympus Station's communications relay and patched in on their end rather than through Parliament's—meaning they couldn't disconnect Vasar from the discussion. Lady Layala stood beside him, and his arm was around her waist.

"Prince Vasar? What are you doing?" asked Krill with an angry shriek.

"Ambassador Krill, maintain a polite tone with royalty," admonished the primary minister. Then he returned his attention to Vasar. "I appreciate your concern, but I don't believe this matter is under your purview, Minor Royal Prince Vasar. We're currently addressing an issue with the Crown Prince."

"Vasar is very much involved in this, as is Lady Layala." Nykal didn't miss the nod from Layala, confirming she was on board with their plan. "We've discussed it, and we decided Layala will accept Vasar as her husband, and he's going to become the next Crown Prince and future King. I abdicate my title."

Pandemonium erupted, and no one thought to mute their side this time. The babble of voices—a mass of confusion, panic, and anger—assaulted their senses as Parliament spent the next five minutes protesting and trying to shout down the idea. Krill was also screaming, and he was so orange that Nykal was almost surprised he hadn't yet had his heart burst in his chest.

When the comm finally settled, the Primary Minister opened his mouth to protest. "You—"

Nykal didn't give him a chance. "I believe if you refer to the Articles of Secession, I have every right to abdicate the throne and assign someone else with direct lineage to take my place. Believe me, Ministers, we've extensively studied all our options over the past few days, and we coordinated this down to the *nth* degree."

"It's treason," protested Krill.

Nykal ignored him. "You have two options. You can either accept it as a *fait accompli* and pretend you knew all along and are all on board. You can even pretend you realized he was far more qualified and interested in the position than I am—which is true—and embrace Vasar."

"Or?" snapped Srgren.

"Or you can fight and scream, and we can make everything public. It's possible the public will support you, but I bet there's more than one noble family that will sympathize with our side, considering the arranged marriages you force. Vasar would like to talk to you about some changes that will take place, but he's willing to wait until you've all accepted the change and had a chance to adjust."

"See here, Prince Nykal. You can't just threaten Parliament. This is extortion." Srgren was now a similar dark-orange to Krill.

"I'm laying out what's happening, not threatening." Continuing as though he hadn't interrupted, Nykal said, "Vasar and Layala would like to marry as soon as possible, so I'd suggest perhaps you give the quiet ceremony you'd planned to thrust upon me and Layala this afternoon to the two of them instead. Be sure to get lots of pictures, because you're going to want to publicize it if you make the right decision to support Vasar."

Without another word to Parliament, he turned his attention to Vasar and Layala. "Thank you again for your willingness to change and adapt, my brother, and Lady Layala."

Layala graciously nodded her head, and Vasar grinned. "It was truly no trouble, my brother. This change makes me happy, and it ensures your happiness as well."

"Tell him he'll be banished, and there'll be an order for execution should he ever return to our territory." Krill made the demand in a high-pitched voice that caught everyone's attention.

The primary minister looked uneasy. "I don't believe we should go that far, Ambassador Krill."

"You must. Parliament must be strong and declare him an outlaw. He's broken with our ways, all for a filthy human."

Hadley bent forward over his shoulder then. "This filthy human is authorized tell you that Ambassador Krill is no longer allowed on Olympus Station." Hadley said the words in a completely professional manner, though it was obvious she was trying not to grin. "His clearance has been revoked, and the next ambassador who arrives will be carefully vetted and personally approved by Prince Vasar and Nykal before gaining admittance."

The primary minister grimaced, apparently realizing he didn't want to get on the bad side of the Coalition or Olympus Station. While their planet's satellites had rare precious metals, so did dozens of asteroids and other uninhabited planets in their galaxy. They were more inconvenient to reach and required setting up mining operations, but the Coalition had far less to lose by expelling Jroj than Jrojans, though it probably wouldn't come to that after mediation. The Coalition would be more likely to impose trade sanctions that would strangle the economy of the planet.

Nykal could practically see those thoughts crossing the primary minister's face. The older man's shoulder sagged, and he turned pale orange as he swayed before straightening. "I believe your plan is a sound one, Prince... I mean, Mr. Atole. Crown Prince Vasar will be most welcome, and his impending marriage to Lady Layala is cause for celebration. Ambassador Krill will remain silent about what's happened, or he'll face the consequences."

Krill let out a strangled sound of shock at the primary minister's words, but he didn't retort. His frill sagged pitifully against his head.

"Of course, you will be welcome anytime you wish to visit Jroj, being the brother of our future king. And your consort will also be welcome to visit." The primary minister looked like he was choking on a large object as he said those words. He sounded like it too.

"Thank you for your graciousness, Primary Minister and Parliament." His voice was heavy with irony. "Hadley will be enjoying the status of my wife, not consort, but I'm certain there are times we'll want to visit my brother and his lovely wife. I wish you all luck."

He disconnected the connection to Parliament before they could. Krill disappeared as well, since he had been on their signal. That left him and Hadley to communicate with Layala and Vasar, and they did for a few minutes as they firmed up plans. Once more, he expressed his gratitude to both of them before ending the connection. "I'm sorry you had to experience that."

Hadley frowned. "To be honest, I expected it to be far uglier and hear quite a few aspersions thrown my direction."

He smiled softly. "They probably muted that part."

She laughed as she leaned forward, and he leaned back. She settled on his lap, clearly content with the position. "I love you, Nykal, but are you sure this is what you want?"

"It's definitely what I want, and there's no going back anyway. Believe me when I say I won't change my mind. I've never wanted to be the king, and Vasar has a much better disposition for the task."

"And he gets to be with Layala, who actually knows your brother and clearly has an affection for him as well."

"It doesn't hurt that she also has an affection for being the queen, but Vasar realizes that. He's confident *viiraria* will grow between them as well."

"I'm sure it will." She snuggled closer, laying her head on his shoulder. "You won't need to claim refugee status, but I'm sure Commander Templeton will have no problem issuing you a residency pass if you'd like to stay here on Olympus Station with me."

"I wouldn't go anywhere else, my love. Wherever you are is where I belong." He pulled her down to him as she lifted her head, and he bent his to meet hers in a fierce kiss. The kissing escalated, and their hands roamed freely over each other. It seemed like no time at all before she was above him, her sheath tightening around his shaft as he pressed fully into her.

She was so beautiful in her ecstasy, and he knew it was a sight of which he'd never tire. Hadley was his mate and the future mother of his child. Perhaps *children* even, and for the first time in at least ten solar cycles, and probably longer—since he realized at a young age that being part of the Royal family was more prison than pleasure—he was optimistic about the future.

He didn't know what he was going to do with himself just yet, but he had the heady freedom of finally figuring that out based on what he wanted, and not what Parliament or others decreed. Most of all, he wanted Hadley, and he'd found a way to be with her. That ensured he'd be happy regardless of what other directions his new life might take.

Epilogue

THREE SOLAR CYCLES later

"How was your first day as a senior oxygen scrub tech?" asked Hadley as she returned to their shared quarters after her shift.

Nykal smiled. "It was satisfying. I'm good at it, and I get to work with my hands."

She grinned and sat on his lap, where he waited for her on the couch. "You are good with your hands." As they crept up her body, she purred in satisfaction. "You always have been."

Their interlude came to a screeching halt with the sound of, "Mama, mama," as little Mygal came down the hallway at a run, likely alerted to Hadley's return by the sound of her voice. He'd been in his room playing, and his sturdy frame entered the living area a moment later.

He threw himself into the mix, climbing onto Hadley's lap, where she sat on Nykal's. She hugged both of them tighter, basking in the happiness she got from her little family. She pressed a kiss to Mygal's peach-colored cheek, once again admiring how beautiful his skin was. It was a perfect blend of the two of them, but he didn't have any of the black striping characteristic to the Jroj. He hadn't seemed to notice or mind, and she thought he was absolutely perfect the way he was.

So was his father, and she couldn't resist leaning forward to give him a kiss as well. It wasn't the innocent kiss she'd pressed against Mygal's cheek. This one was more intense and passionate, the kind of kiss that could quickly get out of control—if they hadn't had their toddler on their laps.

He wiggled and bounced. "Can we go to Sin-ewe-vo?" He slightly mangled the pronunciation of Senufo, but in an adorable fashion.

"I do have some time booked for the VR platform." She winked at her son, amused by his excitement and Nykal's. Even after three solar cycles, Nykal still enjoyed their weekly visits to the VR platform. They'd explored many other places during that time, but they always came back to Senufo. He found it as peaceful as she did, and Nykal liked to play in the shining crystal waters.

As they stood up to make the trek to the VR platform, she held both their hands. They were about to enter virtual-reality, but there was no way it could compete with her actual reality. There was no match for the love she'd found with Nykal, and the product of their union, sweet little Mygal. Hadley was happy, and she seemed to get happier every day.

About Aurelia

AURELIA SKYE IS THE pen name *USA Today* bestselling author Kit Tunstall uses when writing science fiction romance. It's simply a way to separate the myriad types of stories she writes so readers know what to expect with each "author."

Did you love *Alien Prince's Secret Baby*? Then you should read *Security Agent's Alien Bartender*[1] by Aurelia Skye!

[2]

Agent Emily Ipsy is determined to make a name for herself. That leads to unauthorized shifts and sneaking around. She keeps running into Anthracite, the bartender. If he's really just a bartender, why is he everywhere—and why can't she stop thinking about him?Anth is stationed at Olympus Station on assignment from his government. He's there to do a job, but Emily keeps getting in his way. She's maddening, distracting, and pure temptation. He needs to keep his eyes on the job and hands off the security agent, but that's proving impossible. When an old enemy of his people surfaces, he'll need Emily's help to find out why Baatesh is there and stop what he's doing. After working with her at his side, will he ever want to let her go?

---

1. https://books2read.com/u/mvZLQX

2. https://books2read.com/u/mvZLQX

Also by Aurelia Skye

Alien Baby Pact
Baby For The Brundle Commander
Baby For The Grimlock General
Baby For The Palantir Chief
Baby For The Alphan Captain

Celestial Mates
Wrong Place, Right Mate
Destined For The Drakari Warlords

Cybernetic Hearts
Mated To The Cyborg General
Claimed By The Cyborg Commander
Fated For The Cyborg Officer
Meant For The Cyborg Captain
Baby For The Cyborg General
Cybernetic Hearts: Complete Series

Dazon Agenda
Written In The Stars
Alien's Babies
Diplomatic Affairs
Moon Madness
Across The Stars
Emperor's Assassin Bride
Dazon Agenda: Complete Collection

Future Fairytales
Hooked

Harrow Bay
Hell Gates & Hot Flashes
Nightmares & Night Sweats
Warlocks & Wrinkles
Love Spells & Liver Spots
Phantasms & Presbyopia
Vampires & Varicose Veins
Mermaids & Mood Swings
Séances & Sagging Skin
Necromancy & Knee Pains
Marids & Memory Loss
Devil Deals & Dizzy Spells
Happy Endings & New Beginnings
Harrow Bay, Volume 1
Hellhounds & Mistletoe
Harrow Bay, Volume 2

Sweet Escapes
Hook & Wendy

Three Crones Inn
Vastly Inn-proved
Ghastly Intentions
Ghostly Inn-heritance
Three Crones Inn Compilation

True North
True North #1: Death & Deception
True North #2: Rescued & Revelations
True North #3: Fire & Ice
True North #4: Enemies & Lovers
True North #5: Truth & Tiranog
True North #6: Fight & Flight
True North #7: Love & Loss

Wounded Warriors
Relentless
Marked
Justice
Wounded Warriors Collection
Hunted

Standalone
Reluctant Companion
Princess By Mistake
Fire Lord's Assistant
True North
Dragon Laird's Witch
Alien General's Rebel Consort
Tempted By Demons
Enemy Combatant
Grotesquerie
Mistaken Bounty